THE TRIAL OF
Ebenezer Scrooge

THE TRIAL OF

Ebenezer Scrooge

Bruce Bueno de Mesquita

The Ohio State University Press

COLUMBUS

Library of Congress Cataloging-in-Publication Data
Bueno de Mesquita, Bruce, 1946–
    The trial of Ebenezer Scrooge / Bruce Bueno de Mesquita.
        p. cm.
    ISBN 0-8142-0888-6 (cloth : alk. paper)—ISBN 0-8142-5086-6 (pbk. : alk. paper)
    1. Scrooge, Ebenezer (Fictitious character)—Fiction. 2. Heaven—Fiction. 3. Trials—Fiction. I. Dickens, Charles, 1812–1870. Christmas carol. II. Title.
    PS3602.U84 T75 2001
    813'.54—dc21   2001002105

Text and jacket design by Paula Newcomb.
Type set in Trump Medieval by Sans Serif, Inc.
Printed by Thomson-Shore, Inc.

9 8 7 6 5 4 3 2 1

Contents

Preface

I ENDEAVOR in this ghostly little tale to uncover the good that lies hidden in even the worst of hearts. My story is meant to be read with tongue lodged in cheek, but not too firmly.

The tale of Ebenezer Scrooge's life and transformation at the hands of three Christmas spirits is so much a part of British and American culture that few contemplate whether Scrooge or people like him really warrant the harsh treatment they receive in life and literature. Alas, we are more likely to know Scrooge through movies than through the written word. Movie renditions of his story unwittingly reveal how good a man Scrooge really was. Each movie invents scenes to establish Scrooge's best-known alleged flaws: his miserliness and his coldhearted indifference to the welfare of others. For instance, the superb 1951 movie shows Scrooge rejecting more bread in a restaurant because it costs ha'penny extra and turning away from his nephew Fred because Fred's birth caused the death of Scrooge's sister Fan. Neither scene, nor the "facts" they portray, appear in *A Christmas Carol.* I have written this little book to reveal the truth about countless privately generous people like Ebenezer Scrooge.

Through *The Trial of Ebenezer Scrooge* I recast his story to reveal its similarities to the life of Faust. Scrooge lived an exemplary life until he was visited by the Ghost of Christmas Yet to Come. Relying on evidence found within the body of Dickens's great work, I hope to help raise our awareness of how quickly and unjustly we may judge others, responding to rhetoric and innuendo at the expense of the facts. If I succeed in that, I will be happy indeed.

May my tale possess your thoughts pleasantly throughout the holiday season and all the year.

Acknowledgments

———

IT IS MY DELIGHT to acknowledge the patience and assistance of the many friends who have tolerated the development of my little story. I particularly thank my former colleagues at the University of Rochester and my current colleagues at the Hoover Institution at Stanford University. They, as well as my family and friends, have tolerated the telling and retelling of my version of *A Christmas Carol* every Christmas season for as long as I can remember. They have borne this burden with good grace and humor. Their patience and clever insights have haunted me daily. May all of their days be filled with as much joy as they have brought to mine.

I wish also to thank Mr. Charles Dickens. I have taken the liberty of using his language where it has helped to serve my cause. May the reader be pleasantly engaged in discovering Mr. Dickens's own high regard for Ebenezer Scrooge.

——— CHAPTER ONE ———

WHEN last we cast our weary eyes upon Ebenezer Scrooge, it was Christmas day 1843. He was a man transformed. No longer the miser known to all of London town, Scrooge was now a good and gentle man. He had given his word to those long-ago ghostly visitors whose coming Jacob Marley had foretold, promising that he would dedicate the remainder of his worldly days to making our journey on this earth a gentler, kinder, happier one. And Scrooge was better than his word. He became as good a friend, as good a master, and as good a man, as the good old city of London knew, or any other good old city, town or borough, in the good old world.

We look back now on Scrooge in the last few days of his mortal life. The cold snow and blustery wind remind us that Christmas is fast approaching: Christmas 1856. We meet Ebenezer Scrooge, now a very old man indeed, as he makes his way through the dreary lanes of London town. We climb with him to the top of Ludgate Hill, being careful of the children sliding joyfully down the frosted street, and look down upon the snowy fields of St. Paul's church-yard. There, surrounding Christopher Wren's great edifice, we see a myriad of Londoners going about their merry business upon the eve of Christmas. Just in front of the great church's steps is gathered a gaggle of people who are mercilessly taunting an ancient biddy.

"A penny fer some cheer, a bone fer me dog. A penny fer some cheer, a bone fer me dog. A penny fer some cheer, a bone fer me poor dog," was the endlessly repeated chant of the ragged old hag, herself made up of little more meat than one might find on just such a bone. Her croaking voice, emerging from the steps of St. Paul's Cathedral, was drowned out by the unkind looks and harsh quips tossed her way by some of London's finest folk as they made their way down Fleet Street to the Middle Temple. Few cared enough to make even a trembling donation to the pot laid down just by the bared teeth of her mangy, protruding ribs of a beast; a dog that looked as though it had better be given lunch soon lest it mistake a passerby for a tasty morsel. Scrooge, as he did every day at this time, worked his way through the sneering crowd, never fearing beast nor hag, to give the lady a shilling and the dog a scrap of food and a sympathetic tickle under its chin. Though he did not enliven this ritual today with a smile—he never did—neither did he forsake the beggared woman and beast.

"God bless ye kind sir, God bless yur goodness and damn these miserable creatures here what gives me nothin' but grief and pain." Ebenezer did not pause to take in the woman's praise or to hear her curses but rather continued on his slow passage through the town. Even as the old crone called out to Scrooge, promoting his salvation, others—gentlemen solicitors and barristers called to the bar, gentlemen who sat in judgment of their fellow beings—decried his generosity, fearing his was just the weakness that would assure the decline of the British Empire. Scrooge paid them no mind either. As he made his slow and steady way, he popped an occasional raisin into his almost smiling mouth.

On this particular and fateful evening, Scrooge's meandering took him toward a narrow lane, a cold corner of London well known to him during his days as proprietor of Scrooge and Marley, Moneylenders. In but a few minutes' time, quite nearby St. Paul's, Scrooge found himself in the midst of a small, frosted crowd, a few members of which passed in and out of a humble pub, the venerable George and Vulture. Scrooge, lurking in the shadows in order to remain unseen, contented himself by listening to an exchange between a few hoary gentlemen who stood in the pub's doorway, arguing the precepts of their religion.

"What greater charity can the good Lord have had in mind," said one stout, red-nosed fellow, "than to assist some unknown, un-

washed, needy soul; a soul who can offer no recompense but gratitude? It is a blessing indeed to give to such a soul as that."

"The best charity is a sturdy kick in the arse! Let them needy
beggars work like honest folk and not bother me, that's my answer
to you, good sir!" retorted a middle-aged gentleman who was holding a great tankard of beer in one hand and a jangling purse in the
other. "What need have they to be poor and bothersome in a land of
such wealth and opportunity as this? No sir, if they are poor it is because they choose to be so."

And so the argument went back and forth, with no progress
made but in the wealth of the innkeeper who kept these gentlemen
in their cups. The drinkers tarried long, pursuing their debate with
much good cheer and energy. None seemed in such a hurry that a
moment of repartee would be sacrificed to job or familial duty.

Their animated debate and clanking of tankards were unexpectedly interrupted by a solitary, meager voice, choking back the cold,
embarrassed by her misery. On her knees, young Molly begged for
charity from the gentlemen at the George and Vulture. Molly's face
was dirty. Her head displayed a tangled mass of hair that matched
the dishevelment of her plain, torn dress. Those in the crowd who
cared enough to notice her at all observed Molly's unkemptness
with such disgust that they did not see the kindness shining in her
eyes or the gentility in her youthful bearing. But they could not escape the frail cries of the small child clutching at her bosom.

"Oh good, kind gentlemen, spare a little compassion for my
poor child's soul. Can you find it in your hearts to give us some
small trifle for food; just a penny or two, but a penny or two? Anything, please, anything for my little angel this Christmas Eve." No
response did she receive. "Something for my wee babe. She is so, so
cold."

Molly, on her knees, her head cast down in shame, one hand
stretched out in humiliation, the other grasping her little daughter—
the rapidly dimming light of her life—interrupted the debaters of
fine religious precepts as they milled about like birds of prey waiting
for the flicker of life to depart some poor soul.

Going from gentleman to gentleman, tugging at their jackets,
she pleaded. "I ask nothing for myself, but my dear little one, oh

Lord, please help. She is nothing but an innocent, helpless baby. Look at how pretty she is, how good and brave." Molly propped up the frail, tired child, who opened her sleepy eyes a little wider. "Eppie dear, smile for the gentlemen, sing a little joyful Christmas carol for them. Show them how you appreciate their kindness and generosity. They take pity on you dear, I know they do. I know it. Christmas Eve, it is Christmas Eve." The girl, obeying her mother's wishes, sang with all the sincerity her little body could muster, "God save ye merry gentlemen, Let nothing you dismay."

Eppie's song faded with the crowd. In apparent obedience to the song's refrain, undismayed, they turned away from the starving mother and her listless, half-frozen little girl. The gentlemen flew away from Molly and into the beckoning warmth of the pub or along the snow-laden paths that would carry them home. They could no longer tarry where, but a minute ago, time was the cheapest thing they owned. The man with the jangling purse broke off his discussion to return home to his family. His haste was only exceeded by that of his stout companion, who had a sudden remembrance of duties that could not be postponed an instant. As these good gentlemen dashed off to the cares of their own lives, Molly pleaded, "Oh please, won't you even look on her sweet face and golden hair? I'll sell a lock for ha'penny. A ha'penny is all, a ha'penny to save her soul."

But the milling drinkers and arbiters of charity dispersed in a twinkling, leaving the poor mother and her withering little child alone in the narrow alley just by Raveloe Lane, the snow pelting them in the face, Molly's outstretched hand empty of even one solitary coin. Alone, that is, except for Ebenezer Scrooge. Mr. Scrooge remained, emerging from the shadows when all others had departed to their homes and hearths. He was neatly dressed in a greatcoat, with a muffler flung carelessly around his neck, worn in so loose a manner that its ineffectiveness against the cold was ensured. Scrooge was thin, his features severe yet not unkind. Though he was very old in body, his eyes sparkled with the innocence of youth, as if living a life reborn. The crown of his head had long lost any remnants that might prevent the sun's warmth from penetrating to his scalp, but the side of his head was covered in long, straight grey hair that fell wildly to his shoulders. His eyebrows were thick and unkempt, being the first-noticed aspect of his worn face. Their bold fullness stood in sharp contrast to his thin, aquiline nose. His lips were thin, too, and bore a bluish cast—perhaps from the cold, perhaps from long-established habit. Old Scrooge must once have been tall, but he stood now stooped forward. His steps were slow, as is the wont of many old people. Yet in him slowness and crookedness of form seemed to come less from any infirmity of body than from an infirmity of spirit, as if he were careworn from the aged life he had lived. His gait and demeanor resembled those of a beast of burden harnessed to some great, ponderous, inescapable chain.

Scrooge, hearing Molly's sighs and touched by her pitiable state, unwound the worn muffler from his neck and offered it to her. His ancient hand was long, thin, and reddened from exposure to the frosty air. Its white fingers and brittle, yellow nails proffered the muffler with a steadiness that belied his hoary state or the severe chill that must have settled within his bones.

"There, there, dear, sweet young mum. Tseh, tseh, dear me, you have but newly outgrown being a child yourself. Let me help you, please. My scarf will do you more good than it has ever done me, I am sure. Won't you take it? I declare, it will wrap your little girl three times round." At this thought the old man smiled softly, almost as if he felt awkward with his own goodness. Searching his pockets for the source of Molly's salvation, he at last, and much embarrassed, declared, "Goodness, forgive me, I do not have even a penny on my person. Dear me, what am I to do? Ah, but here—just a moment's time and I will help you."

Scrooge scribbled something on a tattered piece of paper. "Take this note and go straightaway to the old moneylender's shop. You'll know it at once. It's only a few streets from here.'Scrooge and Marley' is painted on the window, dear girl. Go there, go straightaway and see the new proprietor. Go there and ask for Fred. Give him this note from his uncle and he shall find you lodgings and a good job, my poor, poor dear. Go at once. It is much too cold for that wee babe to be out at this hour." Scrooge reached out to stroke Eppie's golden hair. "She is such a quiet, sweet, innocent light." Scrooge's eyes became heavy with the memory of his own little sister, Fan, who had died these many long years ago. He looked at little Eppie, but he saw only Fan. "I cannot endure her suffering even another minute." At this Mr. Scrooge, wiping a tear from his eye with one hand and thereby wiping away the vision of little Fan, reached with the other hand into his pocket and produced a small bundle.

"Here, child, take a handful of raisins for yourself and your daughter. Take your fill until you get to Fred's, then he will see to a fine, hot meal and a warm fire for you. Just hand him my note. Tell him Uncle Ebenezer said to take good care of you. Now, be good and go at once—go, both of you. Go to Fred and may God bless you."

"Thank you, sir, and thank God in Heaven that such as you still lives in this world. Little Eppie will remember your kindness always, for all eternity, that I promise you. God bless you, sir." Molly, her lips trembling, said this with such conviction that no one listening could have doubted her sincerity.

Even before these thoughts were fully uttered, old Ebenezer Scrooge, unburdened of his bundle of raisins, made as much haste as his gait would allow and was gone. Not wishing to embarrass poor, mortified Molly, he dared not linger to hear her extol his virtues. How few they had seemed to others, he knew all too well. History had judged him a miserly skinflint and dastardly soul. Still, he walked away smiling and feeling very pleased with himself indeed.

Soon thereafter Scrooge's nephew, Fred, did provide Molly and Eppie with a warm meal and good cheer, sitting them down before a lovely hot fire—so hot, in fact, that little Eppie cringed at the unfamiliar warmth. But he knew of no job that suited Molly. He sent them on their way, sadly knowing that their anguish was no closer to lasting relief. But at least some small comfort had been given to the two, who were but two of the thousands of afflicted souls in London. The scene of Molly and Eppie repeated itself at countless byways and narrow lanes far too many times that Christmas Eve, as it had every other eve the year long for as long as there had been years. There was not always an Ebenezer Scrooge ready to provide warmth and hope for a poor mother and child.

Though Scrooge had helped as much as he could, he could not

do enough to save Molly and little Eppie or the countless other suffering souls nurtured in poverty side by side with Britain's great, burgeoning empire of wealth. Eppie and Molly lived out their lives in hopeless melancholy, never beyond want's door or need's abode. With the rolling of but a few years, the child died—at the tender age of eight, I believe. Her mother, downhearted with despair, fallen from every station in life that she might ever have hoped to attain, took little time in leaving London's cold and joining her child at Heaven's door, where there is always room and bread for the poor.

Scrooge's own brief remaining time in this world was lived out in the meager comfort he had earned through hard labor his life long. He tarried in his earthly form but one more Christmas Eve beyond that long-ago meeting with Eppie, and then he wheezed his last breath upon this earth.

⊰❦⊱

That Scrooge was at last dead and departed from our earth there must be no doubt, or nothing wondrous may come of this tale. His passing was, in its own peculiar manner, a most momentous occasion. Indeed, news of his death traveled through London with a rapidity usually reserved for fallen monarchs or publicly hanged villains. Not that the city's inhabitants were distraught at Scrooge's death. The good and kindly deeds he performed in the waning years of life had not outweighed the memory of his miserly past. No, few were distressed at his passing; rather, they were curious about his affairs. Word of his demise was received with eager expectation among his business associates. Rumors of great wealth accompanied Scrooge in life, never more so than after his storied encounter with the ghost of his dead partner, Jacob Marley. Had not Scrooge, in his declining years, shouldered the burdens of raising the children of his clerk, Bob Cratchit; of saving poor Tiny Tim's life; of giving to every charity that came knocking at his door; and of seeking out those so foolish as to fail to knock? Yes, the good old folk of good old London town were sure there must be a great fortune.

"What has he done with his money?" asked a red-faced gentleman with a pendulous excrescence on the end of his nose that shook like the gills of a turkey-cock.

"I haven't heard," said a man with a large chin, yawning. Left it to his company, perhaps. He hasn't left it to *me*. That's all I know."

Such discussions of the disposition of Scrooge's wealth were commonplace indeed on the highways and byways of London's commerce. Among Scrooge's many business associates who gathered daily at the Stock Exchange or took lunch at the George and Vulture, calculations of the bequeathed riches drifted through the air like some putrefying stench.

"What d'ya think, sir? Will his nephew inherit his fortune? I'll wager a guinea that he will."

"It's a wager then, good sir. You are making a foolish gesture, I'll tell you that. I doubt he would give his fortune to Freddy, truly I do. How could Scrooge turn over his establishment and his wealth to Freddy? Scrooge has always been such a good man of business, while his nephew is a bumbling incompetent. I just cannot see it— no, sir!"

"Well, we'll know soon enough. The will's to be probated in a few days' time. I agree with your sentiment, sir—there's not much ability in Fred. But Scrooge was right fond of him, that's what I'm banking on."

"Excuse me, gentlemen. I could not help but overhear your wager. I wonder if perhaps you would like to enrich it a tad. I should like to suggest that Scrooge will have entrusted his fortune to Mr. Bob Cratchit, his loyal old clerk."

"Come, come, sir," said the first gentleman, "Cratchit is not a man of much imagination and certainly not a man of business. He's not even a gentleman."

"I'll take you both on," replied the second gentleman. "It is my considered opinion that neither Fred nor Robert Cratchit will receive the fortune—that's what I say. Scrooge will have left his money to some worthy, sensible, successful soul. He'll not see it dissipated in foolishness, whether by Fred or by Bob. No, I think we'll find the fortune has gone to a Cratchit all right, but it will be Mr. Tiny Tim Cratchit, not Mr. Bob, and I'll add a bob to the wager on that score."

"Tim Cratchit, eh, the famous barrister? Is he related to Bob Cratchit, then?" inquired the third wagerer.

"Indeed, sir, he's the old man's son."

None of these gentlemen or any others suspected what Tim already knew: that Scrooge had died as poorly as he had lived. There was no fortune to leave behind.

Oh yes, Scrooge was dead. Yet he had not been the man people thought he was. He expired his last breath in lonesome solitude, his remains lowered to a pauper's grave in a far and vacant corner of some long-forgotten field. No lunch was served the mourners, nor any gift imparted to the well-wishers who came to bid him farewell, though these were the customs of the day, for none save one were there to record Scrooge's passing. Scrooge died as he had lived—an outcast, misunderstood by most who shared his time and place. Among all the many who noted the end of this notorious life, only Tiny Tim recognized in Scrooge the good and kind man that he was and ever wished to be. Only he was moved to mark this death as the loss of a kindred spirit. No other cared enough to notice Scrooge's generosity. Not Bob Cratchit, though he was often the beneficiary of Scrooge's philanthropy; not Nephew Fred, though his own good fortune owed much to Scrooge's intercession; not the old hag and mangy dog at St. Paul's, though both would be much the poorer for this man's absence; not even Mr. Charles Dickens, though his continued fame among the young is most assuredly indebted to the character he gave Mr. Scrooge.

Scrooge passed in solitude to the world beyond the grave, the world that he had witnessed briefly in life. He perished content with the life he had lived, the deeds he had done, the kindness he had bestowed on his fellow travelers through their progression to the grave. Scrooge died with a humble faith that he would find at last the peaceful rest so elusive to him in his mortal form.

Such repose seemed entirely right to him. In death Scrooge foresaw only that eternal bliss which must, by rights, follow upon a hallowed life. That he had lived a good life, he was sure; that those in Heaven would be blind to his goodness he had never believed. Yet the chill had but newly crept into his body, the cadaver had not yet found its way to the grave, when Scrooge's spirit learned that his kindnesses were overshadowed by the image his creator, Charles Dickens, had struck of him. Repentant in outward appearance but

believing that he had been always innocent within, Scrooge had labored to fulfill the wish of his long-dead partner, Jacob Marley, that
Scrooge escape his fate. Now, however, that the prospect of the court
of heavenly justice confronted Scrooge, he feared that his exertions
for good might not have been enough. Though he believed, without
excessive pride, that his failings had been few, it now was clear that
his soul, like Jacob Marley's, could face unremitting torment. As
Jacob had foretold, there would be "No rest, no peace. Incessant torture of remorse."

෯

Transfixed by fear for the future, Scrooge's soul wandered through
the outer reaches of the other world for six score years and more,
knowing neither rest nor comfort but suffering neither pain nor privation. Through his meandering journey, Ebenezer observed man
and spirit in places of joy and of suffering; but mostly he dwelled
upon the places of suffering. Wherever he went, by whatever path or
through whatever town, always he saw specters wandering hither
and thither in restless haste and moaning as they went. Every one
of them wore the chains they had forged during lives of depraved indifference to their fellow human beings; some few were linked together; none were free. Many had been personally known to Scrooge
in their lives. He had been quite familiar with one old ghost in a
white waistcoat who cried piteously at being unable to assist a
wretched woman with an infant whom it saw below upon a
doorstep. Though it wished to intervene for good, Scrooge's old acquaintance had lost the power forever. This old ghost's affliction,
reminding Ebenezer as it did of the charity he had given poor Eppie
and countless others like her, made Scrooge feel strangely happy
and hopeful for his own soul. Surely he, who had been kind and
good to beggar woman and child, would not suffer the piteous fate
of the white-waistcoated ghost. Surely!

In this way, by wandering and observing humanity and spirits,
his breast filling with benevolence and compassion, Scrooge began
to understand the world he had left and the world whose entry he
sought with the greatest fear and foreboding. And always he hesitated before knocking at Heaven's gate, waiting for a sign that

might instruct him about the fate of his soul, waiting for the salvation promised by Marley's ghost or the damnation threatened in the countless retellings of his tale every Christmas Eve.

At last, feeling that his soul's education was complete, Scrooge, his courage gathered up, sought entry into Heaven. He was eager to finally resolve his fate. And so we rejoin Scrooge now as his old, grey, stooped form walks through the weighty gates of the Court of Heavenly Justice; the ethereal court that is solely empowered to set aright all wrongs, no matter how long ago committed or how seemingly just in their age. Here Scrooge's life will be judged. Here the sins that were Scrooge's crimes in life will be weighed against whatever goodness and kindness he rendered his fellow man. Here Scrooge's soul will be condemned, pardoned, or reclaimed for Heaven. Here he will know for what purpose each human being lives out life and what is judged worthy of reward, punishment, or redemption.

As Scrooge's apparition passed beyond the prodigious gate, with trembling, solitary steps and slow, he saw for the first time the court where his own destiny would be determined.

"Oh this is a ponderous, wondrous court," thought Scrooge, smiling and intrigued. Talking to no one in particular, he observed, "I've never seen the likes of this court, the magnificence of it." And then, his voice falling to a whisper and his body trembling with fear and awe, "My lord, what power is it that resides in these hallowed halls? What dreams of salvation must be dashed here, without hope of appeal or pardon!"

Scrooge looked about most carefully, acquainting himself with the awesome powers of the Court of Heavenly Justice. One such power particularly attracted his earnest attention. The chamber possessed the most extraordinary ability to instantly transport all within its bounds to any scene or situation, whether forward or backward in time, given the slightest hint that such conveyance could prove beneficial to justice. Scenes from Scrooge's own life veritably flashed before his eyes.

"Hello, boy," shouted Scrooge at the child image of himself. No sooner had he seen the apparition than it disappeared, almost as if he were riding a merry-go-round. Scrooge cringed to see himself standing there, once again an old man. But then just as quickly there he was, an apprenticed young clerk rejuvenated in the office of his old employer, Mr. Fezziwig, and then just as suddenly he saw himself as master of his own moneylending establishment. Scrooge saw his past self in moments of joy and of sadness, and always engrossed in his own affairs.

Awed by the tribunal's purpose, Scrooge's spirit made his way through the poorly illuminated marble hallway of the great palace of justice. He came after a time to the far end, where a lone desk broke the monotony of the room. At this simple desk sat an officious clerk who registered Scrooge's arrival. Although the date was well into the twentieth century—long after Scrooge's death—the clerk dressed and functioned in the style of Scrooge's time. Whether he did so from some desire to make his wards more comfortable with their surroundings or just as a result of long-established habit, I cannot say. That Scrooge felt reassured in approaching so familiar a clerk, however, there can be no doubt. The clerk, entirely disinterested in Scrooge, turned the yellowed pages of the great ledger before him. At last finding the entry "SCROOGE, EBENEZER: 1774–1857," he lifted his quill pen and placed a mark next to the name. Having completed this task, the clerk, shaking the last bit of ink from the nib of his quill back into its well, looked up at Scrooge. Pointing to one end of the hallway with an outstretched finger, he noted, "Your arrival has been expected, Mr. Scrooge. Indeed, you have kept the court waiting too long." Following the finger's lead, Scrooge haltingly proceeded to the doorway that took him to the court's main hall, where his soul's trial would begin.

Moving slowly, finding himself suddenly enveloped by a great chain as if he were a common criminal or an already condemned shadow of his past self, Scrooge made his way through the court. As he moved forward, dark, sinister shades poked him and pawed him, pulling and tugging on the chain he carried. They taunted his spirit, breathing wretched, putrid, sulfuric ether upon him. The meanspirited ghouls sniped and thrashed, tripping Scrooge, forcing his immortal essence to come crashing to the ground, cutting at him, tearing at the flesh of his body and any hubris remaining in his soul. No sooner had they knocked Scrooge down, his head striking hard against the stone floor beneath, his chains cutting through his flesh and covering him in blood, the links pressing hard against his old bones, than the demons pulled him up and threw him down again. Battered by these devils as he made his way down the path, he tried to fight them off, waving his chain-laden arms madly through the air, but they seemed to ooze forth in ever greater numbers from within his very being, their essence mingled with his own.

Sickened though he was by their stench—pained, bloodied, and frightened by their presence—still Ebenezer Scrooge remained un-daunted by the devils or by his new confinement within the links of chain foreseen by his long-dead partner, Jacob Marley. Confident of his salvation, Ebenezer pressed ever forward, his eyes scanning his new surroundings with a keen and eager look. He was pleasantly surprised to now discover himself in the company of other spirits than the loathsome demons. All around him were souls that had come to witness his judgment. Scrooge set his eyes pleasantly on the gallery of spectators, themselves all apparitions of mortals de-parted. Seeing them invigorated his own pained spirit. He noticed that these happier spirits were set off from the court's main cham-ber by a balustrade with intricately carved pillars. Just beyond them lay a small section of the gallery that was obviously reserved for im-portant personages—or rather, the immortal essence of such per-sons. To Scrooge's disappointment, that area was empty for the nonce.

As he passed further into the court, his tribulations diminished. The ghoulish creatures that had attacked him receded within his own essence again. Freed from their torment, he took in his sur-roundings. As he looked about, joy filled the lacerations of his heart. Now he could see what the court's spectators could see. Overhead arched a spectacular mahogany ceiling, coursing its way upward to a glass dome through which the light of all life shines—a light that eased his pain and healed his wounds.

Forward of the gallery and surrounded by the grandeur of ebony panels bathed in light stood grand oaken desks, one to the left and one to the right of the great podium at which the chief justice of this greatest of courts would sit. At one desk sat the famed Professor Blight, lately of Oxford. He was scheduled to speak on behalf of all who believed in Scrooge's sinfulness. It was he who would prosecute the charges brought against Mr. Scrooge.

Professor Blight (who, inexplicably, was always given his title when addressed) was a tall, full man, not at all like the gaunt figure of old Ebenezer Scrooge. Eschewing the conventional wig typical of those called to the bench, Blight wore his glossy black hair, as always, slicked down, shining like a wet lollipop. The viewer's eye, struggling to appear not to notice, was drawn inexorably from Professor Blight's hair to the pendulous excrescence on the end of his prodigious nose. Blight had grown accustomed to such sideways glances long ago and had learned to ignore them, avoiding excessive embarrassment to the viewer. He was known to be jovial among friends—enjoying a joke at someone else's expense more than most men—and to be hard as nails with those who opposed him. Many a barrister was said to have given up the bar after encountering Professor Blight. Many have commented on how well his name described his station among those called to the bench.

A small, frail soul was seated by the other desk. His countenance bore a contemplative calm, as if captivated by the agreeable thoughts of childhood. Though his form was not that of a child, he nevertheless reminded onlookers of the warm innocence of that time in their own lives. This diminutive figure, the shadow of Tiny Tim grown into adulthood, would present the argument for Mr. Scrooge—or rather, for Mr. Scrooge's soul.

The court had provision for a witness's box and a narrow dock, with one plain oak chair, in which the accused was to stand or sit. A large door in one corner supplied the way to an antechamber from whence would come those who were to testify before the court. Their words and expressions would be weighed by the one judge this court has ever known. No jury was needed; no peers could understand or consider the evidence more fully or more fairly than this judge. Neither was there a stenographer in this court; none was needed. All who attended the court were certain to recall each word and to judge and be judged strictly in accord with the evidence that was given. If fairness abides in the universe, it was here that it made its home.

Scrooge was approached by a large apparition, the bailiff of the court. He escorted Scrooge's spirit to the dock for the accused, opening the narrow doorway to allow him access. Scrooge hesitated at the threshold. His bright eyes cast about from one corner of the court to another, and then—the ghouls within him having returned to their accustomed place, his head held high—he entered. He was at last ready to put his wanderings to rest and confront his fate.

Mr. Dickerson, the bailiff of the court, stepped away from Scrooge's box and came forward to commend all within his hearing to rise as the Judge of All entered the courtroom.

—— CHAPTER TWO ——

SCROOGE looked keenly upon the judge. Oh how joyous and terrifying was this spirit's form! Massive, its head covered with a flowing white mane, its hands delicate but powerful, calloused and chafed with the familiarity of hard labor, the judge was awesome, in every aspect remarkable. The judge's garments were surprising in their earnest simplicity. Neither elegant nor refined, they were the humble clothing of those who till the fields or toil in the coal-laden bowels of the earth or scrub the scullery of the well-to-do or build great edifices—the clothing of any who earn their bread by the hard labor of mind and body against the oppression of mankind and of nature. The judge's profile— elderly, wise, vigorous, and caring but unbending before injustice— projected the nurturing of motherhood and the trustworthiness of a grandfather. Many meeker souls looked away from the judge, its bright countenance too extraordinary for their sight. Yet it sought to turn men toward it and never turned away from any who sought its comfort.

The Judge of All spoke. Its voice—for truly we cannot say His or Her voice—was sonorous, robust in its demand to be heard. The sound, though never loud, filled everyone's consciousness, leaving no room for even the slightest digression.

"We are here assembled on the gravest of matters. A soul's eternal future is to be determined by what transpires among us. Let every spirit come to this tribunal honestly and forthrightly that only truth may prevail. Ours is a most onerous task. We confront a spirit deemed throughout ages to be a greedy, grasping, cold, hard, and miserable wretch. But *we* do not know him to be so or not to be so. This it is our task to determine. Ebenezer Scrooge is charged with willful indifference to his fellow beings; of coldhearted, miserly greed without care or concern for those less fortunate than he. He stands accused of being a cold, tightfisted, hard, cruel miser. If true, he must be cursed with eternal damnation; if false, we must determine whether his was an exemplary life deserving of salvation and entry into Heaven. The principal accuser is the late author of Scrooge's life, Mr. Charles Dickens. He declares the defendant to be the most unfeeling, unbending, uncaring being in his own great realm of creation. I ask now of Professor Blight that he summarize for this court his understanding of the charge and of Mr. Cratchit that he summarize the essence of the defense this court is to hear."

Professor Blight addressed the court and the spectators gathered to witness the end of Ebenezer Scrooge:

"Honored judge, esteemed guests, witnesses, and wretched accused, I come before you this Christmas day to inquire what muse or Christmas cheer can bring us here assembled to consider the salvation of Ebenezer Scrooge? What contemplation can make us believe a worthy cause exists for this evil scourge, this detestable curse on humanity? Oh in life he was a covetous old sinner, this man Scrooge. He was far too ghastly ever to earn forgiveness or the eternal bliss of salvation. Never did he care for his fellow beings. Never did he show them pity for its own sake, never was he generous of spirit without calculation of its gain for himself. Never did he seek to bring a human touch to his business dealings. Never did he think how he might make another's life less burdensome. Never!"

The speaker, becoming more animated, continued: "He positively took pride in his coldhearted withdrawal from his fellow men and in their fearful withdrawal from him. A solitary blight who drove all human contact from him with wanton joy—this was Scrooge. What did Scrooge care? It was the very thing he liked. To edge his way along the crowded paths of life, a shadowy figure warning all human sympathy to keep its distance. As wicked and despicable a soul as his has not often been known in mankind's all too sorry history. But for it to have been known at all is too often. He is and has ever been a miser; a taskmaster; a friendless, fiendish, insufferable beast; a meanspirited wretch who would deprive a child of a penny simply for the pleasure of seeing the deprivation. This we know of him.

"Ebenezer Scrooge is deserving of no forgiveness, for he shows no remorse; he is deserving of no consideration, for he granted none. His life was lived in selfish pursuit of his well-being with never a thought or deed motivated by feelings of kindness toward others. No space from the cradle or from the grave can be great enough to undo the misery that he sought to convey to his fellow beings.

"Faithful judge and learned friends, be not misled—as I know you cannot be—by saccharine appeals to mercy and sentimentality. Yes, it is true that even Scrooge, near the end of his life, performed an occasional act of charity—but only out of concern for his own eternal burden and rarely with a thought for those truly in need."

Blight, his voice rising as he reached the summation of his opening remarks, continued: "Scrooge's life was worn harshly. The creases and ridges he shaped in his mortal fabric were not easily smoothed by a few good passes with a hot iron. Only eternity is long enough for this vile soul to contemplate the good he could have done but did not do! Scrooge has filled the book of judgment with the cruelties and horrors he lavished on his fellow beings his life long; now he must reap the suffering he has sown."

Saint Dunstan, sitting in the gallery, was most particularly pleased at the thought of Scrooge's metaphorical iron. He positively laughed out loud in endorsement of Scrooge's condemnation, only to be silenced by a stern look from the judge.

As Blight retired to his seat, the small spirit of Tiny Tim, ready to present Scrooge's case, crippled in bodily form but grand and glowing in his goodness, came forward to address the assemblage. With a voice delicate but not weak—indeed, one that commanded the attention of all, the tiny phantom made his opening speech:

"At this the time of the rolling year, when liberal hearts lavish pity upon those sufferers of the world's privations, seek—oh kindly judge—that spirit of indulgence that reclaims for good the soul of Ebenezer Scrooge. For the span of two mortal lives and more, his memory has been wrenched from goodly thoughts and forced to live in the sordid soil of scornful reflection. An evil soul, so we were taught. Unkind in every contemplation and deed that must be man's lot to endure from him. A slithering beast of a spirit, cruel and cold to his fellow men as they journeyed life's painful course. This is the Ebenezer Scrooge whose acquaintance Charles Dickens presented to us. Scrooge seemed like a man to be hated, not pitied; to be despised and banished from the greater kindness of the Christmas Spirit; the unforgiven rebuke of his age.

"But surely we can be more caring, we of a more compassionate age. Can we not see in Scrooge a saintly soul torn from his faith and his trust; a man born of misery, nurtured in the bowels of loneliness and despair, bred on the abusive temperament of his fellow men?"

Shouts of "No! Never!" from the spectators.

Tim, undaunted by the gallery's interjection, continued: "I shall prove that Ebenezer Scrooge was a man of compassion, of high spirit and generosity. I say, woe to those who have borne false witness these many years against this son of Abraham and forced his now-dead spirit to worship at an idol's altar. For we shall *prove*— not merely intimate, but truly prove—the saintly goodness of this wretched pariah, this man made leper by ages of blind ignorance and misunderstanding! Never too late to put a soul to rest, we entreat the court of eternal mercy to hear our cry and heed our proof; to treat with tenderness the crime of Dickens but to undo the harm born of greed and gain that has these long years been borne by Ebenezer Scrooge."

Tiny Tim modestly, almost sheepishly, resumed his seat, and the judge again stood at the high podium to address all assembled within the great court.

"Much has been said against Scrooge for ages past. Whether evil was done by him or to him is the determination that must be rendered by this tribunal. We stand here eager to do so; eager to right any wrong, whosoever may have committed it. If evil was done, the deed shall remain hidden no longer. Before this highest court shall be paraded those who were witnesses to the crime, those who looked on in innocence, and those whose participation was enlisted for the feat. Each will testify truthfully as to the character of

Scrooge and his acquaintances. Some may fear the consequences for their own souls and so must know now that no punishment will befall them if they testify freely and truthfully of what was said and what was done, of how they felt and what they knew. We shall not layer upon their earlier wrongs their wish to wrong again out of deference to their previous sins. For the sake of the wonder that can come from this tribunal, all must be assured of our pardon and our grace. Far greater is he who saves one soul unduly banished from Heaven than he who proves the exile of thousands."

⊰✦⊱

"My lord, I call Mr. Charles Dickens, most lately residing at Gad's Hill, earlier of Regent's Park, London, and Villa Bagnarello, Genoa, to testify before this tribunal," declared the bailiff, Mr. Dickerson. Thus was the inquiry convened.

Mr. Dickens came forward, his fob watch suspended from a substantial gold chain, his raiment most elegant. His suit was of the finest material, the outer coat lined with elegantly quilted satin, the suit jacket superbly tailored to complement his figure. Mr. Dickens's cravat was held in place by a magnificent diamond brooch. He was a sight to inspire poets; a man of theatrical presence, a whirlwind of self-contained energy.

The gallery gaped in awe to see the phantom of the great man they could not know in life. Only from one lonesome corner came weak hisses, identified with some former literary associates of the great author. Scrooge, standing in the dock, fettered in a ponderous chain, shaking hardened raisins in his cupped hand as if they were iron dice, recoiled in fear and fell back into his chair as he recognized Mr. Charles Dickens. There was no joy for Scrooge in their reunion, of that we can be sure.

"Mr. Dickens," began the spirit of Tiny Tim, "you are called here on a most severe matter. Need I remind you of the fate that has befallen Mr. Scrooge, a man brought to his condition by the fruits of your pen? I ask you now and seek your considered response—do you admit to having given Mr. Scrooge his life and essence?"

"Let there be no doubt of this. I, and I alone, am father to my characters, Mr. Scrooge included. And, sir, need I remind you that you too were given the possibility of immortality by my pen? Even now, though you are free from my authority, you cannot help but know that it was I who created your very being and made possible your presence here today!"

"And," continued Tim, ignoring this declaration of paternity, "do you not charge this man Scrooge with being a tightfisted hand at the grindstone, a squeezing, wrenching, grasping, scraping, clutching, covetous old sinner? Hard and sharp as flint, from which no steel ever struck out generous fire; secret, and self-contained, and solitary as an oyster?"

"I do so charge and have long done so," replied Dickens. "Indeed, your lordship" (these words were spoken with the rich texture of sarcasm), "you honor me with your knowledge of the character of this character. No more unkind and uncaring a man has there been than he. Truly, nobody ever stopped him in the street! No beggars implored him to bestow a trifle, no children asked him what o'-clock, no man or woman ever once in all his life inquired the way to such and such a place of Scrooge. None was so base as he! None more despised or more deserving of that sentiment."

"None, Mr. Dickens? Surely you do not presume to judge this man. Surely you dare not cast him out as a sinner merely on your own authority, you yourself born a mortal!"

"I do, sir, I most assuredly do! You might wish me to deny Scrooge's failings. I will not! To do so would be to deny the very essence of the Christmas Spirit, which must, to do its good works, have weak and sinful creatures to set aright. I will not excuse Scrooge, and I pray that this court will not either. Mortal though I have been, I am the father of his spirit and I tell you he was a sinner through and through, the rightful object of those Christmas Spirits who haunted him long ago. *They are well known to me, and I tell you, they knew him for a sinner.* I aroused their interest, but *they* pursued Scrooge for his own good and for ours. Thank God for that!"

No sooner had the witness given this testimony than a wondrous creature, later identified as one of the very Christmas Spirits who had haunted old Scrooge, chided Dickens most intensely. "There are some who lay claim to know us, and who do their deeds of ill-will, hatred, envy, bigotry, and selfishness in our name, who are as strange to us and all our kith and kin as if they had never lived. Remember that," said the spirit, its eyes piercing the witness, "and charge their doings on themselves, not us."

The witness, ashamed of the pride he had shown in his own powers of creation, nervously fingered the chain of his watch as he attended to this greater spirit. But shaken though he was, he was not ashamed of his charge. Dickens repeated that he knew Scrooge for a sinner—for a cold chill cast on human dealings.

"Perhaps I speak in ignorance when claiming to know the needs of the Christmas Spirit, but I speak not in haste nor in ignorance of the spirit of Ebenezer Scrooge. I cannot deny the wretchedness of Scrooge. He was a covetous sinner. This I know, for I made him so."

"Thank you, Mr. Dickens. We will stipulate for now your faith in having fathered a sinner. But then we must ask—forgive me, sir—why are we to blame Mr. Scrooge and punish him in eternity for that which you freely admit you have done to him?" asked Tim, the specter leaning heavily on his crutch.

"That he sinned needs to be so, it is true, if my story is to bring pleasure to others. But does such a consideration justify Scrooge's lifelong neglect of his fellow beings? No, sir, we cannot excuse Scrooge merely because another set the stage. It was he and he alone who acted with such malice and coldhearted indifference. How can we forgive that man who has come to represent the very basest in humanity merely because another molded the clay? Did I not also instruct the ghost of Jacob Marley to enlighten Scrooge that the common welfare was his business; that charity, mercy, forbearance, and benevolence were, all, his business?" responded Mr. Dickens.

Cries of "Hear, hear!" emanated from among the spectators. Mr. Dickens seemed well satisfied with himself as he folded his hands in front of him and rocked back and forward on his heels. "Yes, I created the sinner as God made Eve; I placed temptation before the sinner as God placed the apple on the tree of knowledge; I gave the sinner the chance to repent his greed as God gave Adam the chance to refuse the forbidden fruit. Like Adam, Scrooge chose to fall, succumbing to his desires and bringing suffering everlasting to his own soul. Were we to blame God for Adam's bite from the apple? Were we to excuse all sin because the Creator made sin possible?"

The prosecuting attorney, Professor Blight, nodded approvingly from his desk at the witness's quick and convincing retort. Mr. Scrooge, much moved by the heavy burden placed upon him by Mr. Dickens, looked away in shame and mortification. Any who could see into his eyes—though few could—were sure to notice that he detested Dickens with a cold, penetrating malice.

Professor Blight, looking warmly and earnestly at the witness, turned toward the judge. "Most esteemed lord, the prosecution has no questions for this witness. We are well satisfied with all he has said and so beg permission that he be excused." The judge assented, and Mr. Dickens stepped out of the box with pleasure painted on his face.

Tim Cratchit asked the bailiff to call the next witness. Bailiff Dickerson summoned Mr. Ali Baba, lately of Arabia, to approach the stand.

As this extraordinary man, with his marvelously jet-black beard and wearing the most colorful of Arabian robes—looking like a character from a pop-up book—entered the courtroom, his huge footfalls awakened long-ago memories in Scrooge. Ebenezer's mood changed from malice to ecstasy with each percussive clap of Ali Baba's step. Forgetting where he was, Scrooge exclaimed, "Why, it's Ali Baba! It's dear old honest Ali Baba!" He waved joyously to his old acquaintance and companion, his chains making an unseemly racket, then—remembering that he was in court and recalling the solemnity of the occasion—sank back onto his bench. There he closed his eyes, a warm smile creeping across his face as he tried to conjure up once again those long-ago days of youth when, alone with Ali Baba's stories and the thousand and one Arabian nights, the young Scrooge had passed the Christmas season.

Tim explained that Ali Baba's testimony would establish the cruel loneliness and abandonment suffered by Scrooge throughout his formative years. Mr. Baba, reinforcing the introduction accorded him by Tim Cratchit, explained his acquaintance with the defendant:

"I knew him well. We visited together over many a Christmas season."

As he spoke, the courtroom turned into a country lane by Scrooge's old boarding school. An expansive meadow of pure white snow, speckled with brown lines of protruding twigs and once-colorful leaves, half buried and turned the texture of crisp slush, made cheery the dismal place to which the court had been transported. There sat the young Ebenezer Scrooge on a half-snow-covered bench, a well-worn book held in his hands as if it were a dear companion. Wafting on the chilly wind, wending its way through young Ebenezer's hair and across the entire scene, was the fading voice of Tiny Tim Cratchit, which was heard to inquire, "What sort of boy was he who grew into so coldhearted a man?"

"Giddyup, Valentine—come on, boy—hurry up there," called the shadow of Ali Baba.

"Why, Ali Baba! Dear old honest Ali Baba, hello there!" shouted Ebenezer across the far-stretching meadow of smooth snow.

"Come, Valentine—hurry up now to Master Scrooge. Giddyup, you old nag! Look at the poor boy, Valentine. He seems such a solitary child; such a melancholy lad this Christmas season, alone but for his *Arabian Nights*. Why, Valentine, I declare his school is all but orphaned at this joyous time of year; the poor boy has been abandoned by his friends."

Valentine neighed in seeming agreement.

As Ali Baba spoke to his faithful horse, he urged Valentine on with his spurs. In short order horse and rider reached their destination, pulling up beside Ebenezer, having pocked the meadow with crescent-shaped horseshoe holes and having had a jolly time doing it, you can be sure.

Scrooge, turning a page of his book, looked up and greeted Ali Baba. "Why, dear old Ali Baba—how good of you to visit me, and on Christmas Eve, no less. Why, I positively would have thought you'd be busy making snowmen in the Arabian sand by now, ha, ha."

"I am frosted enough, dear boy, without your reminding me of the warm place from which you have conjured me. I see that this Christmas Eve you are alone again."

"Not at all," declared the tattered, abandoned young shadow of

Scrooge's childhood. "Are *you* not here? Come—let's not just sit here gossiping and watching this glorious day go by. Let's go riding together."

Ebenezer climbed aboard Valentine, sitting bareback behind Ali Baba, who laughed uproariously as Scrooge's little fingers tickled his jelly belly, the boy trying to hold on for dear life as Ali Baba, Scrooge, and Valentine cavorted through the snowy meadow. Young Ebenezer seemed positively joyous as he lifted one hand ever so gingerly from Ali Baba's belly, shifted his weight ever so cautiously lest Valentine should slide out from under him, and reached into his pocket for a prodigious handful of plump raisins. With a careless pleasure, young Ebenezer threw fat raisins in the air and listened for their *thwat, thwat, thwat* as they punctured the snow.

"And your friends, boy, where are your school chums?" asked Ali Baba, reaching with one hand to snatch raisins from the air like a child trying to catch raindrops in his mouth.

"Oh it is Christmas time, you know. They have gone home to their families. But see what fun *they* are missing."

A cold wind blew just then, freezing the very moisture upon Ali Baba's beard. Ebenezer shivered, perhaps from the cold, perhaps from the knowledge that no hearth was filled with a warming fire in expectation of his coming home that Christmas season.

Ali Baba, a man larger than life, sighed heavily in the box, wrenching the scene back to the courtroom as he shook his head and entire body with the remembrance of those long-past days. With every quake of his dispirited essence, buttons popped from Ali Baba's monumental chest, their tingling on the ground providing some relief to his otherwise melancholy testimony. Then, quite unexpectedly and almost violently, the witness rose, turning away from the attorneys, and looked directly at Mr. Dickens, who had retired to the quiet corner of the gallery reserved for notables. "There he was," and Ali Baba shouted the next phrase as if it must be heard as far away as America, "*alone again,* when all the other boys had gone home for the jolly holidays."

Mr. Dickens tore his eyes from the witness. Just as Ali seemed ready to continue, Professor Blight objected to his testimony. Oozing unctuous contempt, he argued that "Mr. Baba is stating only hearsay and personal conjecture. He is wrongly and maliciously leading some"—and as he spoke he turned toward the gallery, leering at those who had clearly come to jeer at Scrooge's famed creator—"yes, some, my most gracious lord, to fault Mr. Dickens when it is Scrooge's soul on trial. We cannot continue to allow such hearsay and defamation to be heaped on the prosecution's witnesses. Let Mr. Baba remember who is on trial and who is not. His testimony must be restricted to that which he knows and that which he saw! We must not tolerate his unfounded saccharine sentimentality that invents a suffering childhood for the despicable Scrooge."

The judge, without emotion, said, "But Professor Blight, it is well known that Ali Baba's description of the abandoned young Ebenezer Scrooge is not hearsay at all. The very words he used just now were Mr. Dickens's own original description of Scrooge's youthful Christmases. What could be more pertinent to Scrooge's later character and condition than an understanding of the hapless circumstances of his youth?"

Ali Baba, emboldened, continued, reflecting on how kindhearted the young Scrooge had been. As he spoke, the courtroom filled once again with the images, the smells, the very essence of Scrooge's recollections from his school days, disclosing a long, bare, melancholy room. The scene, but a few years later than the first, was one of abject degradation and solitude. The sounds of rotted plaster falling to the ground and leaking pipes dripping water on the barren floor were principal among the interruptions of Ali Baba's narrative. Scrooge's school chilled the bone even more than could be explained by the dead fire within its grate. In one corner sat the young Ebenezer, bereft of a trunk or even a bundle within which to pack his clothing for the approaching holiday. Scrooge's youthful countenance betrayed a smile and projected inner peace and even warmth in that cold, cold place. He watched in silence, unnoticed by his friends as they witnessed their trunks being carried forth from the schoolhouse.

"Be careful there, porter. Put that up gently. Yo ho there, driver—yes, yes—you, driver. There'll be a handsome tip for you if my trunk rides directly beneath your feet, safe against all ills,"

declared one well-to-do, drippy boy. Like all the other lads packing
for the holiday, this boy, though Scrooge fancied him to be a friend,
was too distracted by thoughts of home and of plum pudding to give
any notice to his lonesome companion.

Another boy, hoisting his trunk to the very top of the coach, was
warned by the scarecrow of a schoolmaster to "take care now, Randall, or you'll hurt your back and make it sore. What will your
mother think of the care I provide then, eh, boy?" Randall, with a
good laugh, exclaimed, "We'll all be a good deal more sore at journey's end than I can ever get lifting one paltry trunk, I'll tell you
that. Anyways, coming home all sore and stiff is the least I can do
to give my mum something to dote over, ain't it?"

Much toing and froing there was; lifting and setting down;
laughing and toasting one another's good trip, God speed and happy
holidays. But still alone and unnoticed sat young Ebenezer Scrooge,
content to watch his youthful companions prepare for a pleasurable
holiday and taking more pleasure from watching them than anyone
might have imagined. Certainly more than he could hope to take
from the lonesome Christmas that lay ahead for him.

As Scrooge's unseeing companions made ready to board coaches
and carriers, shaking one another's hands with much huffing and
puffing and toasting of the season, Ebenezer drifted over to young
Master Randall and handed him a little bundle. "A gift for you,
Randall. Open it Christmas morning, won't you? And a happy holiday to you. You are my dearest friend, and I shall be most happy
knowing that you will think of me a little on Christmas day." Randall, quite amused by the strange fellow, said, "Look here, boy, I
must be on my way. Don't be bothering me, will ya." He opened the
bundle then and there and munched on the raisins Scrooge had
given him. Scrooge beamed with pleasure.

Ali Baba's voice drifted through the scene, as if in a whisper:
"Oh you should have seen his joy at the beginning of every Christmas season, sharing the happiness of his friends as they made ready
to go home. How often I asked myself why he rejoiced beyond all
bounds to see them! Why did his heart leap up as they went past?
Why was he filled with gladness when he heard them give each
other 'Merry Christmas' as they parted at crossroads and byways for

their homes? What was Merry Christmas to Scrooge?" Then, tears catching on the mountains of his cheeks, he exclaimed, "Out upon Merry Christmas! Poor Ebenezer! What good had it ever done him?"

"And yet," Tim observed, the scene instantly departing Ebenezer's childhood and returning to the courtroom, "Scrooge was joyous at Christmas. Though these dark hours of his youth were the time of his greatest loneliness, he felt joy for the happiness that Christmas brought his friends. The time delivered only despair into his heart, and yet he expressed sincere joy. A remarkable boy!"

Ali Baba rose again, the bailiff restraining him as he looked malevolently at Dickens. He said, "You, who fathered that poor boy; you were too cruel and heartless. It was you who abandoned him, you who left him desolate at the very time when others embraced their kith and kin in joyous celebration. You did no other than try to crush his spirit for your own sordid gain."

Professor Blight began to rise but saw he need not when Bailiff Dickerson, a persuasively large and serious man, pulled down hard on one of Ali Baba's corpulent arms as the judge instructed the witness to be seated.

Tim, his eyes riveted on the spectators, said, "Has not Mr. Dickens said that he fathered Ebenezer Scrooge? And had not Scrooge's father been cruel in surrendering his son's care to a school that was in deep decay; to a headmaster that cared not at all for Master Scrooge; to a life of rejection?"

Tim continued, "Must we forgive the father? Was he simply incapable of loving feelings? No unkindness did he show to Fan, Ebenezer's dear sister. She had not been similarly discarded, left to struggle in an unfeeling world. No, this cruelty was a specialty of his in treating the young boys of his creation. Who can forget the tragic childhoods of Oliver Twist, David Copperfield, or young Ebenezer Scrooge?"

A certain Mr. Murdstone objected from the gallery, "No one ever mistreated young Copperfield. I object to such a portrayal, I object, indeed." He was ignored and Tim continued:

"And who can forget the obstinate torture of poor Ebenezer? Even when Fan's pleas to let Ebenezer come home finally persuaded

Scrooge's father to relent, still he did not go to his son. Still he sought not forgiveness nor even any reconciliation. No! He sent sweet, young, innocent Fan to fetch her brother home; he could not be troubled to do the job himself. As God had not troubled Himself to save Isaac, sending an angel instead to stay Abraham's hand, so Scrooge's father sent his own angel of mercy. But Mr. Dickens is not God, and poor Fan could not be as strong as an angel! How did he dare entrust his son's future to little Fan, putting so much burden on this small child and so much sorrow in the heart of Ebenezer? Here was true cruelty and callousness for which Mr. Dickens has laid full claim. Blight knows it; I have known it since my youngest days; all of you in the gallery surely must know it too. Yes," and Tim turned toward Charles Dickens's ghost, "even you, Mr. Dickens, have always known it."

One lonely voice rose in defense of Charles Dickens. "Whatever the circumstances of childhood, still, responsibility for the life that has been lived and the sins that have been committed must rest with the man if his soul is ever to be reconciled to its fate." It was the voice of Ebenezer Scrooge, who continued, "Whatever the character of my childhood, Your Lordship, I do not seek salvation out of pity and charity. I have done no wrong in life, and *that*, nothing else, must be the basis of my redemption. Can we not move on to such evidence as will establish . . ."

The judge, not as a magistrate but as a mother ministering to her child, gently interrupted: "Now then, sir, really—you mustn't speak out of turn here. These gentlemen, Mr. Blight and Mr. Cratchit, are quite able indeed. Please then, let us leave the course of events in their able hands. They, Mr. Scrooge, must be the ones who determine the direction of argument and testimony. You must restrain yourself, however difficult that may become from time to time. Their duty is to serve justice and yours is to await their summons."

Scrooge fell silent, but he knew that not a few souls in the gallery had been softened toward him by his intercession. They could not see the cold, calculating malice that resided in his eyes.

Professor Blight stood up as soon as the judge had finished, not to rebuke Scrooge but to cross-examine the witness.

"Mr. Baba, you are quite right to draw the court's attention to the wretched suffering of Scrooge in his childhood. A terrible thing, the way the children of Britain's golden age were plagued by their country's pursuit of gold. No one—but of course I need not remind this court—was more appalled by this condition than the most esteemed Mr. Dickens. But, sir, was Scrooge truly so afflicted? Yes, his younger days were sadly passed in lonesome abandonment. But not for long, and the suffering was well compensated in the days that followed. Remember the words of his beloved sister Fan . . ."

And there she was within the court's view, a little girl barely reaching her brother's shoulder, standing with him once again in his old deserted school upon the eve of Christmas. She was as pretty and kind a little girl as you could ever imagine seeing. Her face blossomed with freckles, a field of flowers in sunshine. It fairly matched the blooming meadow on her dress.

Scrooge, seeing Fan again after so many unhappy, lonesome years, struggled not to sob. He wanted to hold his composure for the sake of preserving the chance to watch her. But the trembling of his lip and the sniffling of his nose gave away his sentiments as surely as if he had cried like a baby. Here in the image of this little girl, Scrooge saw the good that could come from the reclamation of his soul. To be with Fan again, brother and sister, loved as he had not been loved for all these years past—that was the hope and chance for which Scrooge waited. That was the desire of his heart and soul that melted the ice in his veins and quenched the fire in his eyes. In his mortal life Scrooge had been deprived of her love. She had been a tender child, a delicate creature whom a breath might have withered and, alas, had withered in the very awakening of her womanhood. But oh—she had a large heart! How he longed for the heaven of her company.

On this very day of Scrooge's youth conjured before the court, Fan's heart was positively erupting with renewed hope and joy as she spoke to her poor, forsaken brother: "Father is so much kinder than he used to be that home's like Heaven! He spoke so gently to me one dear night when I was going to bed that I was not afraid to ask him once more if you might come home; and he said yes, you should; and sent me in a coach to bring you. And you're to be a man and are never to come back here; but first, we're to be together all the Christmas long and have the merriest time in all the world."

"Home's like Heaven," repeated Blight, erasing the images of Fan, young Ebenezer, and the lonesome school until they were all dwindled into nothingness. "We're to . . . have the merriest time in all the world." These words burst explosively from Professor Blight, reaching every recess, every nook and cranny of that great courthouse. The chamber echoed with little Fan's repeated sentiment: "Home's like Heaven . . . like Heaven . . . like *Hea-ven*."

"Like Heaven, Mr. Baba, like Heaven! What do you say to that?" Ali Baba, disgusted with Professor Blight and feeling disconsolate and dejected, rose to leave the court. As he departed, he turned back and shouted a final, pitiful defense of Scrooge: "You wretches cannot see, you cannot feel, you cannot . . . just cannot . . . ," and then he dissembled into the mist as he left the courtroom, unable to speak the words that wrenched his heart.

Ebenezer did not notice the changed atmosphere of the court or even hear Ali Baba or bid him farewell. He clung through the mist of his eyes to the fading image of little Fan. As she disappeared from view, Scrooge remembered for a moment the loving looks of little Eppie by Raveloe Lane, and he smiled.

⸎

The tribunal having adjourned for the day, Scrooge left the courthouse alone, as was his accustomed lot, by a bleak side door. With great effort he bore his fetters more openly and honestly than most men and made his way to the downhearted cottage that served as his residence during the trial. The streets he passed were indistinguishable in their gloominess. The gutters ran in a trickle to the half-frozen wintry river that divided the town. A solitary boatman provided transport from one bank to the other. Rare was the occasion when even he made the crossing. Scrooge did not seek out this boatman or his barge but rather took the long way around, over bridge and down chilled streets. The houses along the way were no better than Scrooge's own cottage, wanting that care which makes even a ramshackle bungalow into a warm home. Not a board was painted, except with flaking chips of ancient, worn-away care. The people within were likewise worn, not so much from a lack of care as from an absence of caring.

After an hour or so Scrooge arrived at his hovel intent upon a hot bowl of gruel. Gruel had served him well in life, being the mainstay of his Christmas feasting for his final two score years and more, and he saw no reason to abandon the habit now. But disappointment was his abiding companion. Even hot gruel was denied this outcast.

Scrooge shook the snow and slush from his boots. As he entered the cabin, stooped over a little more than was normal even for him, his thoughts were firmly fixed on a warm bowl. But there was no fire within Scrooge's hearth—if such we can call the lowly grate within his abode—with which to heat his thin porridge. A young child not much more than eight years of age, with golden hair and cheerful demeanor, worked happily and willingly as his guardian servant. She was busying herself about the fire, toting full shovels laden with ash. But strange to say, she seemed to bear the ash to the fire, not away from it. It was her apparent duty to thus fill his grate in the evening, dousing any ember that had cared to live the day long. This little golden girl did her chore well. Her day was spent merrily quenching any source of warmth or amusement that might lighten Scrooge's burden. She had no other companion than her thoughts of the future and her happy memories of Ebenezer Scrooge. His was the lot of a sufferer and hers was to insure that Scrooge's destiny would be fulfilled. She made him suffer and yet pleased him, too. Scrooge delighted to look upon her, not only because of the sweet, innocent charm with which she was amply endowed—the sweet innocence that was a daily reminder of his own sweet sister, Fan—but especially because of her enchanting golden hair. How he loved to run his cold, grey, bony fingers through her rich curls, watching the locks tumble between them like coin of the realm. Ah, how well it reminded him of the golden idols of his youth.

"Eppie," said Scrooge, "come, join me in a bowl of porridge. I've brought some honey and raisins to sweeten yours." As she seemed to demur, Scrooge went on, "Don't worry, my dear, I will take mine cold and thin. Perhaps you have not so fully stolen the warmth from my coals. Perhaps there is still time to make your porridge hot." Scrooge spoke to his little servant girl with no malice, no sarcasm, no feeling other than genuine good cheer and warmth. He could not do otherwise. Eppie commanded a good feeling from others by her own purity of spirit. She had commanded such from Scrooge since their very first meeting.

Eppie was good to her mother's promise never to forget Scrooge's thoughtfulness, not even through all eternity. Only the best of souls would have left heavenly bliss to willingly endure Scrooge's fate forever just on the chance of doing him some small good. This Eppie had done. She had given up the companionship of other children; the joyous warmth of her mother in Heaven; even, perhaps, her own salvation—all on the chance of repaying Scrooge's long-ago kindness. Only the basest of souls could have felt indifference to this little sprite. Scrooge felt no such thing.

"Oh thank you, Uncle, but I mustn't, you know. Anyway, I have had my porridge already. I sweetened it just the way you showed me. I soaked yesterday's raisins in rum and honey and poured it on my porridge. Oh how it cheered me and made me warm. I am so sorry that I could not wait for you, but I must not leave any chance, you know, that your coals will still be hot. It is my duty. But soon, Uncle Ebenezer, very soon we will eat hot porridge together and forever."

"Yes, of course, Eppie, my good little angel, of course." Scrooge downed his cold bowl, spooning out his anxieties in a steady, marked cadence, spoon after spoon after spoon until, at last, the cold gruel was gone. All the time that he ate Scrooge watched the little girl, more warmed than if his porridge had been hot off the fire.

"Uncle Scrooge, will you read to me tonight from our favorite storybook?" asked Eppie. "It would make me so happy. Will everyone live happily ever after, Uncle? Oh will they?" Scrooge, unsure of the right answer, struggled to nod in the affirmative for the pleasure it would bring Eppie. "Really, Uncle, oh really—read to me right away."

"Certainly dear, I will read to you. I also want to know if it turns out well, for my own sake as well as for your pleasure. But not just now. We must be patient. Some gentlemen will be calling this evening, and I must attend to them. When they have left, there will be time enough to read."

Though disappointed, Eppie did not argue. Together they washed the porridge bowls and the pot in which Scrooge's gruel had been prepared. Each felt warm and content as the two completed these domestic chores. After a short while their quiet pleasure was interrupted by a knock at the door.

Eppie, hearing the knock, retired to her own room, which adjoined the parlor. Ebenezer, alone with his thoughts, entreated the callers to come in. They did so with alacrity. There were, it seemed, two gentlemen. Eppie could see neither.

Immediately, the voice of Tiny Tim could be recognized among the greetings wafting in the air. Tim grasped Ebenezer's hand warmly—it was the only warmth in that cold hovel of a parlor now that Eppie had retired from it—and begged permission to be seated. This being instantly granted, Tim rested his crutch in a corner near the cold hearth and sat on a hard wooden chair. The second caller could not be easily discerned. He—if, indeed, we can be sure it was a he—was clad completely in black. The face was shrouded, as was the entire body. Only one long, bare finger on its left hand suggested any corporeal essence to this dark visitor. He—for so we will call the specter—spoke by gesture with the lone, exposed finger, and in this way was more eloquent than Cyrano. But on the present occasion Scrooge's second visitor was silent even to the motion of the finger. Silent he was, but the house filled with a sinister air.

Scrooge and Tim exchanged words too soft to be heard. The rhythm of their whispers caressed Eppie in her room. Gradually, her eyes became heavy with sleep. She awoke to the morning sun. When Scrooge's guests had departed she did not know, nor why they had come. Eppie washed the sleep from her face and began the day's hard tasks. Disappointed though she was that Scrooge had not awakened her to read from her favorite book, still she did not awaken him now. He'd had a trying day, and there would be many more before him. Of that, even this little child was sure.

Scrooge rose about an hour after Eppie. She had already stacked wood in the fireplace, awaiting his departure before kindling the flame. Ebenezer, not wanting to keep her cold any longer, gave Eppie a hug, patted her head of golden hair, and bade her a good day.

It was a bitter cold day, but the sun was shining. This uplifted Scrooge as he made his way back to the court, unnoticed and without noticing any around him. He was deep in reflection on the night's visitors, and this reflection continued even as he resumed his place in the court, having once again suffered the torment of the ghouls within him as his essence proceeded down the long corridor to the room within which his trial took place. He sat down with a cold smile upon his face.

◖✦◗

A surprising knock was heard at Scrooge's cottage door. Eppie, unable to see who was there, was fearful of answering. She was not in Heaven, after all, and many evil, sinful ghouls were about even at this, the noon hour. But a voice called to her and she knew it for her mother's.

"Oh Mummy, Mummy, I'm so happy it's you."

Molly hugged Eppie and gave her a big kiss. They sat down together to a hot bowl of pea soup and bread. Eppie had had the soup bubbling on the grate, and Molly had brought the crusty bread with her.

"Oh my dear, it was quite a struggle coming to visit you. I had to battle with so many wretched clerks just to get permission to cross the river over to this side, and then the sinister monsters that one meets on the streets here! My poor dear, how can you stand it?"

"I don't go out much, Mummy, so it's all right, and Uncle Ebenezer is so good and kind. Well, we just have to help him, don't we? Then we will be free of this cold place."

"Yes dear, of course we do, and that is why I've come. In a few days' time a kindly spirit will visit you, a spirit who can help—I'm sure of it. I want you to meet this spirit and do whatever is asked of you. Will you do that for your mummy?"

Eppie hesitated. She was not supposed to do anything but keep Scrooge's cottage. "If you say it's all right, I guess so—but I'm really not supposed to."

"Promise me, Eppie. Do as I ask and don't ask any questions.

When the specter comes, you do as that spirit says—just as the spirit says. Promise me. No matter how things seem, remember that specter will help us save Mr. Scrooge."

Molly's insistence scared Eppie, but of course she did as she was asked. "I promise. I'll do whatever I'm told, Mummy."

"That's a good girl. Now I must be going, and I don't think I'll be back over here anymore. I'll wait for you across the river. Give me a big hug and kiss, you little rag doll. Ummm, I miss you. Oh—and Eppie dear, not a word of this visit to anyone, not even Mr. Scrooge."

"Yes Mummy. I love you—I miss you, Mummy."

⊂⊷⊃

Molly did not return straightaway to the river she had crossed that morning. She went in that direction but a few moments and then turned down a listless street, out of everyone's sight. There she took out a key and unlocked the door of a cottage. The cottage was clearly not inhabited by any permanent resident, and scant signs of life pervaded the premises.

Molly opened a bedroom door, closing it quietly behind her. As the door swung shut, her aspect and character underwent a metamorphosis. The gentle woman of Raveloe Lane quickly faded away, replaced by a different, an earthy and common soul.

A man awaited her on the other side of the door, eagerly looking forward to their meeting. A bottle of cheap brandy rested on a table. She took a swig from it as the man set down his cup and fondled Molly, groping her in a way that your polite company precludes me from describing. She did not pull away or show the slightest displeasure—quite the contrary. With a toss of her head, she used the weight of her body to push him against a wall. I assure you that no time was wasted on whispered sweet nothings or the pretense of caring. Theirs was a business meeting, and they made haste to do that business.

"Tim," she cried, holding her hand out for money. Tiny Tim did not respond immediately. In the height of his ecstasy he forgot whatever cares occupied his soul, submerged as he was in lust. Molly lusted too. She lusted after the opportunity to be with Tim again. Tiny Tim, for his part, did not lust for the fulfillment her body provided; he lusted after her soul.

As quickly as she had come to him, he pulled away, looking upon Molly with contempt. None of the tenderness and innocence that he had displayed in court did he show to her, barely pausing to speak a word. He looked quite content nevertheless as, with a toss of coins, he left Molly to finish the bottle of brandy by herself. He made haste to return to court.

⌘

Dick Wilkins stood in the witness box. Like Scrooge in his youth, Dick had been apprenticed to the moneylender known as Fezziwig. Mr. Fezziwig was widely regarded in his day as the kindest, most generous and spirited of gentlemen. Dick had known Ebenezer well, having worked with him side by side at Fezziwig's establishment until Dick's untimely death upon a long-ago Christmas Eve.

Tim looked gently at Dick and asked him to describe all he knew of Ebenezer Scrooge.

"He was as fine a friend, as generous and thoughtful a lad as I ever knew. I was never more attached to anyone than I was to Ebenezer. In those hard times Ebenezer took my welfare for his own, always without seeking reward or recognition, and protected me from Fezziwig's indignation. Surely I would have perished sooner if it had not been for Scrooge, and just as surely I would have perished later if it had not been for Old Fezziwig!"

Professor Blight, impatient for his opportunity to discredit the witness, interrupted, gesticulating animatedly, his index finger pounding the desk in front of him. "Mr. Wilkins, sir, you have just leveled a charge of great import against dear Old Mr. Fezziwig. Is this the same Fezziwig who generously spent a substantial sum to entertain his employees every Christmas Eve, lavishing them with fine food, drink, entertainment, and general merriment?"

"A curious thing, Christmas with Fezziwig," continued Dick, barely looking at the professor but still clearly committed to answering the professor's question in his own good time. "On the outside it seemed a most festive time when Fezziwig did serve fine punch and good meats and provided pleasant entertainment. I'll not say it was otherwise. But there was a dark side to Christmas with Fezziwig known all too well by those who worked for him."

"A dark side, Mr. Wilkins! Come, come—surely you speak too dramatically. Old Scrooge himself admitted that Fezziwig brought joy to all. Wasn't it Scrooge who said of Fezziwig, 'The happiness he gives is quite as great as if it cost a fortune'?"

"Yes," replied Dick, "but you must remember the whole of Ebenezer's thought. He was admitting how pleasant Fezziwig's Christmas party was for some but at the same time relating the great power for good *or ill* that Fezziwig possessed. You will recall, I am sure, Professor, that dear Ebenezer observed of Fezziwig, 'he has the power to render us happy or unhappy; to make our service light or burdensome; a pleasure or a toil.' That he could do either was learned by hard experience. I am afraid far too often he laid emphasis on the burdensome toil rather than the light pleasure."

"Mr. Wilkins, these slanderous remarks without substance may serve your purpose in bolstering the cause of Mr. Scrooge, but they fool no one, sir. I must urge you to desist from such accusations unless you are prepared to back them up with the relevant particulars," said Professor Blight. He scowled at the witness as he ran confident fingers through his slicked hair.

"I am coming to the particulars, sir! Forgive my being slothful. It is only that I thought the case so well known as not to need elaboration here. If you will it, sir, I shall oblige. I must take care not to do any injustice to Fezziwig, and I thank you for reminding me of my duty in this matter. But neither can I shrink from telling the whole of the truth in this most august tribunal, and shrink I will not. Every Christmas followed the same routine. Each year Fezziwig invited friends, family, and employees to a gala Christmas party. And just as regularly, he compelled Ebenezer and me to labor long and hard for his success. Mind you, we were forced to do the necessary chores without pay because our master's establishment was *supposed* to be closed on Christmas day. That he stopped our wages we did not mind, but that we had to work regardless was a burden, you can be sure."

"What are you saying, man! We all know perfectly well that you celebrated along with all the others." At this hint of a falsehood tunneling its way into the consciousness of the court, the judge gave such a deep grumble as would surely have filled even the most abysmal heart with despair.

"No, Professor—you misjudge. You have not attended carefully to the facts. Here are the key points given to you with exactitude and certainty." Dick, unperturbed, went on to relate the tale of Christmas with Fezziwig.

The lofts and cells of Fezziwig's warehouse wherein his employees sat at their labors became as clear as if the court had been constructed directly upon the spot. The hubbub of commerce within Fezziwig's establishment mingled with the merry sounds of Christmas in the street, accompanying the comings and goings of the fair citizens of London bound for the bakers, the poulterers, and the fruiterers. A clock was heard to chime the seventh hour, and as it did so, Old Fezziwig came back to life:

"Yo ho, my boys!" said Fezziwig. "No more work tonight."

"No work, indeed. What humbug," declared the skeptical shade of young Dick Wilkins. "Oh Ebenezer, what *are* we to do? If I live to be rich like Fezziwig, I will think more kindly on the welfare of my apprentices, I'll tell you that!"

"Come now, Dick, it's not as bad as all that, is it? Old Fezziwig gives us employment, does he not? Then shan't we give him a full day's labor and more if he needs it? It is Christmas Eve after all, and it is only once a year. It's our duty to help out howsoever we can, is it not? That's the way of business, leastwise his business," responded Scrooge, now grown into a strong, straight, and handsome young man of twenty.

"Christmas Eve, Dick. Christmas, Ebenezer! Let's have the shutters up," cried fat Old Fezziwig with a sharp clap of his hands, "before a man can say Jack Robinson!"

Fezziwig, quite comfortable on his stool overlooking Dick and Ebenezer, poured himself a glass of sherry, which he swallowed in one gulp, giving a large and quite inexcusable belch as he set his emptied goblet down on his high desk. There was no warmth of holiday kindness on Fezziwig's face—only the flush of sherry and of authority over two young men who must beckon to the clap of his cold hands, Christmas Eve or no Christmas Eve.

"Snap to it, my boys. This old place must be sparkling in a jiffy if I'm to impress one and all with the generous nature and beauty of the Christmas season. No doubt you'll want to insure that, ha, ha!" cried Fezziwig, his fat jowls shaking like a pudding upon the copper.

Ebenezer, off to one side, implored Dick, "Come on, Dick, quick now, my lad, before Fezziwig finds a more ill temper in that bottle of sherry. Come on! Remember the way we did up the shutters last year? We must do it again, you know. Let us think on what great fun we can have at it. Remember how we charged into the street with the shutters—one, two, three—had 'em up in their places—four, five, six—barred 'em and pinned 'em—seven, eight, nine—and came back before you could have got to twelve, panting like racehorses, neighing the whole time? Really, Dick, I do believe we had great fun."

"Remember! When I have forgotten *that* it will be the death of me. Ebenezer, how can you go to it with such good humor? Fun, indeed! Racehorses, indeed! I can tell you that no racehorse can be happy in its toil. A pair of stupid draft horses, that's what we are. Draft horses to a tyrant."

The long-departed shades of Ebenezer and Dick ran from the dust-covered chamber of Fezziwig's warehouse, leaving marks of their footwork in the dust on the otherwise bare wooden floor, charging ferociously in response to their master's every whim. Soon enough, Dick was covered in a cold, clammy sweat as his breathing became labored in that dank place. Ebenezer, his heart bursting with the spirit of Christmas and with compassion for young Dick, fearing that Fezziwig might think Dick a shirker, redoubled his own efforts to make ready for the great Christmas celebration. The sweat dripped from his chin and brow, forming muddy puddles on the dusty floor, as his body bent crooked under the weight of his toil.

What did Fezziwig care? He, downing sherry and eating sweetmeats, called out task after task to his young apprentices.

"Hilli-ho!" cried old Fezziwig, skipping down from the high desk with agility. "Clear away, my lads, and let's have lots of room here! Hilli-ho, Dick! Chirrup, Ebenezer! Quick, my lads. Time to be moving furniture about. We must clear away to make a dance floor for the fine ladies."

"But Mr. Fezziwig, sir, I implore you. We've already worked a full day. We positively need some rest. A small respite, sir, that's all I ask," pleaded young Mr. Wilkins as boldly as might be.

"A respite, Mr. Wilkins? Indeed, I can provide you with a lifetime of respite. It is still Fezziwig's name on the door, sir, not Scrooge or Wilkins. Ain't that so, Mr. Scrooge?"

"Yes, sir—of course it is. But a minute, Mr. Fezziwig—what harm can there be in Mr. Wilkins's resting but a minute? I fear Mr. Wilkins is not at all well. We'll have your party ready all the faster, sir, if you give him just a minute," implored Ebenezer.

"So, you think it is best for the apprentices to run my business too, do you, Mr. Scrooge? I'll not tolerate this insubordination. I'll have a dance floor for the ladies quicker than you can say Jack Robinson, breath or no breath, and don't you forget it. Now get on with what I tell you or get out. There's plenty of young bucks what would gladly take your places. Get out, I tell you, or clear away!" barked Fezziwig.

Working feverishly, with Dick ready to collapse onto the floor if but a little breeze should catch him in the face, Fezziwig's establishment was slowly transformed from a bleak countinghouse to a place for great merrymaking. But the making of the place certainly was not merry. Dick and Ebenezer feared Fezziwig. Ebenezer, anxious that their mild rebuke of Fezziwig might have gone too far, whispered to young Dick as they ran about like mad hatters.

"Dick, I'll help you, but we mustn't seem to hesitate. There must be nothing we wouldn't clear away or couldn't clear away with old Fezziwig looking on, or it will be the end of us."

"But Ebenezer—dear, dear friend—I cannot continue, I just cannot. When can we rest? I'll die of apoplexy if he does not relent. And you know he never looks away; never chances that we might pause to catch our breath or say what o'clock it is. Never!"

Dick Wilkins was quite right in this. Once the young apprentices had cleared all the furnishings so that every movable was packed off as if it were dismissed from public life for evermore, Fezziwig set them to the next chore, Christmas Eve notwithstanding.

"Hilli-ho, boys! Chirrup! Come, come—on with it, you young bucks. The floor is to be swept and watered, the lamps are to be trimmed, and fuel must be heaped upon the fire. I want this old warehouse as snug and warm and dry and bright a ballroom as you would desire to see on a winter's night." And again Fezziwig, resuming his seat atop the high stool, poured out a goblet of sherry, which he downed in growing ill humor.

"I will finish, Dick—you go rest," whispered Scrooge to Wilkins. Ebenezer uncorked his body, already bent double from the evening's labors, and, looking as tall and strong and ready as any man could, assumed the burden of his own work and Dick's.

The ever-attentive Fezziwig noted Scrooge's redoubled effort. "What's this, Scrooge! Wilkins is too weak to heap fuel upon the fire, eh? Well, you'd best be sure to work as fast as two men, or you will both be out on your ears this very night."

The court was dumbfounded by the scene it had just witnessed. The creaking of boards wrenched them back to the courthouse, where Professor Blight was rocking back and forth on his heels, protesting that Wilkins was not telling all. "You were not so sick, Mr. Wilkins, that you were unable to attend Fezziwig's party, now were you? Did you not then enjoy the reverie that ensued at Fezziwig's expense for hours on end, sir? Did you not gorge yourself at his table and dance until your feet could not proceed further? Did not Fezziwig provide a merry old time for you and for Mr. Scrooge each Christmas Eve?"

"If only it had been so, sir. Others, most assuredly, had a wonderful time. Mr. and Mrs. Fezziwig were filled with joy as well as porter, and their daughters—oh what pleasure they had," replied Dick. Again the court's aspect was that of Fezziwig's business establishment, with a fine table of meats and porter giving off the luscious scents of a Christmas feast. A fiddler's music filled the chamber, and young couples frolicked and danced here and there.

"Wilkins, Scrooge, come stay by my side but a moment," said Fezziwig's specter as it sat close by the table of victuals.

Scrooge and Wilkins, with hesitant care, approached their master, whose face was contorted and red with the warming glow of too much sherry and a touch of porter. "Now, my boys, I want this to be a most memorable Christmas for my guests. You'll do everything you can for Old Fezziwig, won't you, lads? I can count on you to make my party a success, can I not?"

"Of course, Mr. Fezziwig, but whatever can we do to help, sir?" inquired Ebenezer, as Dick stood silently by his side.

"My fine young bucks, I have noted the smallest of embarrassments this evening, which you can most assuredly help me overcome," indicated Fezziwig as he reached out to squeeze the passing, dancing rump of a young lady. She squealed deliciously and, quite red in the face, said, "Really now, Mr. Fezziwig!"

"What might that be, Mr. Fezziwig?" asked Dick, whose tongue had returned in a sarcastic mood.

"The meal, sirs, the food and the drink, sirs. More than fifty guests, sirs. A great expense, sirs. I am afraid my wife has made but a wee error again this year, sirs. We are, in point of fact, short, and I'll not have a guest of mine say that Fezziwig is anything but a most generous man; the premier entertainer of the Christmas season, sirs. Do you take my meaning, gentlemen?" asked Fezziwig, as if there might be any doubt about it.

To make sure his point had gotten across, Fezziwig beckoned young Dick and Ebenezer to take some tasty morsels from a fine tray of meats. Each, professing some mysterious ailment of the head or stomach, declined any food or drink, much to the satisfaction of Old Fezziwig.

Dick Wilkins's voice broke in upon the courtroom as he responded to the prosecutor's inquiry. "No, Professor, there was no joy, no reverie for us at Fezziwig's Christmas party. We were given nothing like the fine feast served at the Cratchit household many years later."

Scrooge waved his arms in endorsement of Dick's testimony, his chains lurching the drowsiest of observers in the gallery back to wakefulness. The rattling of the shackles mingled in Tiny Tim's mind with the fading sound of Fezziwig's clock that used to mark the close of the business day. At the clattering knell, Tim Cratchit seemed to emerge from a trance. He found himself fully restored to the courtroom, no longer drifting between it and Fezziwig's workplace or wherever else his reverie might have conducted him. He thanked Dick Wilkins for his testimony and promised that his statements would not be forgotten. He had done a great service in revealing the truth about Fezziwig and the thoughtful nature of Scrooge, said Tiny Tim. With this, Dick departed.

——— CHAPTER THREE ———

THE court, having listened so attentively to Wilkins's talk of cakes and meat and porter, drew its attention now to filling its own hunger. The Judge of All adjourned the session early and ordered that a great feast be set out for all in attendance. Crystal bowls of hot toddy competed with yellow-white glistening eggnog, ample carafes of sherry and porter, and vast kegs of beer for the attentive favors of the milling crowd of thirsty ladies and gentlemen, witnesses, officials of the court, and spectators all. A suckling pig, a delicious red apple in its mouth, stared out at the guests, imploring them to take but a taste, a morsel of tender lusciousness that would make any mouth water. And the roasts—oh the roasts—so red within, so crisp and crackling without, and floating in their own juices.

Two little boys stood close by the tray of roast beef. One eyed all the passersby as if he were standing guard at a great bank robbery. "Hurry, Timothy, it's my turn now." "Oh hush up, Edward, there's plenty here for both of us. Give me another piece of bread, just one more dip into the gravy and then you can go." "It ain't fair, Timmy, we'll get caught and I won't get nothin'." The boys kept at this endlessly. First one and then the other stood guard while his accomplice dipped a big, crusty piece of bread into the gravy and, with a tremendous smack of his lips, swallowed the bread and came back for more and more and more. No one minded. There was plenty for Timothy and Edward and everyone else, too. Every tray brimmed with the savory scent of plenty, and all ate well.

Mrs. Dilber, Scrooge's old laundress and a resident of the witness list, was washing down a sudsy beer as Mr. Hiram Dewars, an extraordinarily corpulent gentleman, refilled plate after plate with sweetmeats, bread, and chocolates while at the same time stuffing cakes and pastries into his cavernous mouth. As he did so he looked all about him, his tart little eyes leaping from spot to spot as if to make sure that no one would notice the prodigious luncheon he set before himself. He should have enlisted the help of the two young boys who stood sentry one for the other, so as to waste less of his own opportunity in cautious observation of the milling crowd.

Young Oliver Twist, standing in front of a great table that stretched almost endlessly, was picking and choosing among the handsome cakes and cookies before him. Oliver, looking a little green around the gills, plunged into eating enough dessert to keep ten healthy boys content. His old nemesis, Mr. Fagin, standing right by his side, looked quite disgusted.

"Can't I take some more, Mr. Fagin, sir? I'm still hungry," whined young Twist.

"More, Mr. Twist? More? You shall be the death of me, I do believe. A glutton is what you are—now ain't that the truth, my dear, lovely Nancy?"

"Come now, Fagin, my dear. He's only a boy. Let 'im eat to 'is 'art's content. It ain't costing you nothin', is it?"

"He's embarrassing me, he is—why yes, my dear, he is!" said Fagin, and as he did so he grabbed Oliver by the ear and bade Oliver's surname greet his ear with a great Twist. All the while he promised Oliver that he was very fond of him indeed and that all this twisting and arguing was hurting him and Nancy much more than it could ever hurt poor little Twist. In this fashion young Oliver was dragged from the table, but not before his quick little hand made a last foray into the dessert tray to come up with a slab of chocolate decadence.

The interlude offered by the meal provided Fezziwig a chance to speak with Dick Wilkins for the first time in many scores of years. Fezziwig approached humbly and ashamedly, for he was not the man he had been.

"Dick, my poor, poor boy, can you ever forgive a pigheaded old man for being too blind to see, too unfeeling to care, too thought-less to help you after all these years? Believe me when I tell you I am not the man I was. Nor could I ever be again. Forgive me, Dick, forgive me. I implore you, forgive me! How wrong I was, how ill I treated you. Oh Dick, forgive me so that I can know some peace, some rest, and escape the unrelenting torment that is mine all the day long." Fezziwig made this little speech in so doleful a fashion, with his hand resting on his brow, his head tilted slightly ajar in so melodramatic a fashion, that it might well have touched the heart of any man standing nearby.

"Mr. Fezziwig, forgive you, indeed! Why, I bet I can forgive you faster than you can say Jack Robinson," responded Dick Wilkins with a large grin and a hearty laugh.

"Your health, Mr. Wilkins," offered Fezziwig as they each lifted a large tankard of beer to mark the happy occasion.

The meal being completed, all retired from the courthouse to prepare for the next day's events. All save two young lads in ragged clothes who stayed behind to clear away and eat whatever scraps might have been left behind. Scrooge lingered long enough to see these boys, and though he did not speak to them, they sensed in the tilt of his head and the gentility of his small smile the camaraderie of one who had shared their lot.

Scrooge had not partaken of the courtroom feast. He was prohib-ited from doing so but would not have eaten even if it had been his choice. He had long ago decided to content himself with only the simplest of fare. This evening was no exception.

When he stepped outside, prepared for his solitary walk back to his cottage, Scrooge noticed that Tiny Tim Cratchit was still linger-ing in front of the great Hall of Justice. "Tim, my boy, wait a mo-ment there. Will you join me at the cottage again tonight? There is much to discuss of today's events and tomorrow's plan. Bring your friend with you, Tim, the one who came also last night. I am eager for that one's views, too." "Yes, of course, Uncle Ebenezer. We will be most pleased indeed."

"We had, I dare say, a good day today, Uncle Ebenezer," said Tiny Tim as he shed his coat and boots at Scrooge's cottage door. "I do not know which was the better touch, to resurrect Ali Baba yesterday or to bring Dick Wilkins back from the grave today. But surely the court was moved. It went hard on Old Fezziwig, eh?"

"Yes, Tim, that was as fine a gesture as I have seen. To point the finger at Fezziwig that way might well qualify you for the rank of first-grade conjurer. Surely only a magician could so easily turn a lifetime of animosity toward me and love for Fezziwig so topsy-turvy. You are to be congratulated. But what is next, Tim? Can we crush Blight's reputation and be relieved of that turkey-cock of a prosecutor? He is no different now than ever he was. He is nothing but a strutting wretch standing in the way of our great and grand design! Nothing, Tim, nothing must be allowed to defeat us in our quest. I will not tolerate damnation when we can serve such a magnificent purpose!"

Tim, enjoying Scrooge's praise of his performance but a little put off by his efforts to orchestrate their case, observed, "We'll beat them at their own game yet and so more fully advance our cause than any have done before. You can be sure of that! Do not trouble yourself with the how or when of it. Be assured, I have made all the necessary arrangements. Of course we cannot be content with failure. We must win our case. Fear not, Uncle Ebenezer! Tomorrow will be quite exciting for all of us, I promise you!" At this remark the sinister finger of Scrooge's other guest unfolded, outstretched, and became rigid with a dismal pleasure at the thought.

Eppie, again alone in her room, overheard this discourse. She did not know what to make of it. What could they mean? She could not say, but she was troubled not a little by it all the same. Not so much that anything untoward was said or done, but Tim Cratchit's tone implied a demeanor quite different from his reputation, as if there were more than one spirit within his small, lame body. Still, Eppie did not attend overly to the dark foreboding in his tone. She kept busy in her little chamber, lying upon her cot, playing with the sock doll that Ebenezer had fashioned for her but a fortnight before. She hugged her dolly close to her, running her little fingers through the golden tousles of hair that Scrooge had stitched on the sock and, the doll's smiling face staring at hers, dropped in and out of that restless sleep which accompanied her most nights.

After some time the two guests bade Scrooge good night. They left by the front door, melting into the shadowy night as if they had not been present at all. They carried no brightness within them that might lighten the dark.

As soon as they had gone, Scrooge remembered how he had disappointed Eppie the night before.

"Eppie, dear," he whispered at the little girl's door. "Eppie, are you awake still, my precious?"

"Yes, Uncle," responded the groggy little voice.

"Oh dear me, I have awakened you, haven't I? Go back to sleep, Eppie—rest well."

"Oh no, Uncle, read to me, please. I am not sleepy at all, really! Please, please, just a little bit of story, Uncle, just a bit, because I am afraid of nightmares. Ple-eee-se, Uncle Ebenezer."

"Of course, little one. We'll have no nightmares here, now will we? Then do come back to the parlor and sit on my lap while I read."

Eppie bore a troubled look as she rejoined Scrooge in the parlor, but he was too distracted to notice. Scrooge unconsciously ran his hands through her golden locks while in his hardened mind's eye he dwelled on the evening's conversation. He said nothing except, "Let us read now, my dear." Eppie sat on Ebenezer's lap, still clutching her little Molly (as she had named the sock doll), alternately hugging or kissing the doll's face while Scrooge ran his fingers again through her hair then took the great book from which he read down from its shelf.

As he opened the book, Eppie said meekly, "Uncle, is everything going to be all right? Mr. Tim sounded so strange tonight. I'm scared that something is wrong. Promise that you'll tell me if anything bad is going to happen. Promise."

"Yes, of course, dear." Scrooge patted Eppie's golden hair, his eyes softening as he looked at the little girl on his lap. "My dear little one, I will never let anything bad happen to you. Never! Never!"

He pointed to his place in the book. By one steady, sturdy candle's light he began to read. The hour showing that the day was well worn away and sleep still resting heavily upon Eppie's eyelids, Scrooge contemplated reading but a little while. Eppie drifted in and out of sleep as Scrooge read. Although she did not understand or recognize the tale she heard, the story enchanted her still and filled her with awe and apprehension.

In the morning's brightening light that pierced through the broken panes of Scrooge's frozen cottage, Eppie recalled only these few lines, which she comprehended not at all:

> If we say that we have no sin, we deceive ourselves,
>   and there's no truth in us.
> Why, then, belike we must sin, and so consequently die:
> Ay, we must die an everlasting death.
> What doctrine call you this, *Che sera, sera,*
> What will be, shall be? Divinity, adieu!

⟨⊷⊶⟩

Scrooge did not encounter Eppie in the morning. He rose earlier than the birds, took no meal, bore up his chains, and set out down the path that would return him to the court wherein his fate would be determined. His greatcoat was buttoned to the chin, more, it seemed, to keep the cold within him from escaping than to keep the cold without from getting in. He walked alone in a most dignified manner, fettered though he was, hobbled though he was by the weight of the chain he bore and the life he had lived. Many a neighbor came out to gawk at Scrooge, and this gave him some considerable pleasure. Perhaps they would be uplifted by his cause and gain some gratification in his path.

Scrooge stopped only once along the way, at a small shop where he purchased honey and raisins, and then walked briskly toward his destination. He exchanged not a word with anyone, not even in the shop, where he seemed well known.

Scrooge arrived early at the courthouse. Slowly he undid his coat, being careful never to set down the chains he had forged in life. A great gust of frigid air escaped from his cloak, chilling the court, but, of course, there was no one to record the intemperate climate Scrooge carried within himself. Resuming his seat in the stuffy box set aside for the accused, Scrooge awaited patiently the arrival of the day's proceedings. He hummed quietly and smiled contentedly to himself. One small, shriveled raisin was rolled continuously between his thumb and index finger until, worn out at last, he crushed the raisin and threw it upon the stone floor.

In time the court filled with the familiar faces of the judge and bailiff, barristers and plaintiffs, and with old and new countenances in the gallery. The court now reconvened, Professor Blight set out to establish the harshness of Scrooge's character.

"Most honored judge, the next witness, Mr. Hiram Dewars II, will now decisively reveal the woeful, grievous, detestable character of the accused. I ask that he be called to the stand."

Scrooge listened to Blight's statement with utter indifference. His mind was fixed on daydreams of Eppie, who would now be reading her own little book or playing with her Molly Dolly by a warm, bright fire in Scrooge's cottage. He was thinking of her and of Tiny Tim, too, when the name of Hiram Dewars penetrated his musings and called his attention back to the courtroom.

Mr. Dewars, a large man with a still larger chin, came forward in the court. A merchant banker, Hiram Dewars had long been a member of Scrooge's business club and had known Scrooge throughout their respective careers.

"Mr. Dewars, can you tell us what you know of Ebenezer Scrooge that might pertain to his qualities as a man?" inquired Professor Blight.

"I know from personal experience that he was a clever man of commerce. Many was the time I was defeated by Scrooge in our competition for an attractive client by his dexterous dealings in business. He was a man obsessed with the desire for wealth. Greedy, I should say!"

"Greedy?" interrupted Professor Blight. "What makes you choose that particular description? Are there facts to support this inference of yours?"

"Indeed there are, sir. It is well known that Mr. Scrooge occupied himself with business at all hours of the day and on all occasions. Even the death of his partner, Jacob Marley, did not stop his money-making course. Scrooge was not so dreadfully cut up by the sad event but that he was an excellent man of business on the very day of the funeral and solemnized it with an undoubted bargain," responded Mr. Dewars.

"And at his own funeral, were there many so cut up that they abandoned their day of business for his memory's sake, Mr. Dewars?"

"Indeed not, sir! At the time, as I am sure you yourself well remember, I observed that it was 'likely to be a very cheap funeral, for upon my life I don't know of anybody to go to it.' "

At this declaration Professor Blight wiped his brow and then continued his interrogation of the witness.

"Was Scrooge known for a miser, Mr. Dewars?"

"My, my, sir, but of course he was. He was so miserly that no one could stir his heart to charity, not even on Christmas Eve. It was widely commented in his time that he refused to help the poor, and he said of himself that he could not 'afford to make idle people merry.' "

Professor Blight continued in this vein for some time with the witness, summing up by observing:

"The essence of the witness's testimony is that Scrooge was a well-known miser, seeking his fortune without regard to the common or gentlemanly decencies of the age even when it came to dealings of charity and death. So heartless was Mr. Scrooge that even the blind men's dogs appeared to know him, and when they saw him coming on would tug their owners into doorways and up courts, and then would wag their tails as though they said, 'no eye at all is better than an evil eye!' "

As Blight spoke, condemning Scrooge in every manner conceivable, Tim Cratchit prepared to seize the opportunity provided by his worthy opponent. Adroitly, he set out to exploit the secret, long kept, that Dewars seemed to have inadvertently revealed.

"In sum, your most esteemed honor, Mr. Scrooge was a scourge upon humanity; a miser who set no value on human dealings and felt no pity at the sight of human suffering. Mr. Dewars, an intimate of Mr. Scrooge in life, himself a trusted and well-respected gentleman, has plainly and freely testified to these facts. I am done with the witness, as I hope this court is done with Mr. Scrooge. Mr. Cratchit, your witness, if you please." Professor Blight, head held high, flung wide the tails of his coat and turning tail, so to speak, resumed his seat.

Tiny Tim planted his crutch firmly in front of him and, at last resting his chin upon its top, spoke. "Thank you kindly, Professor. With the court's indulgence, I wish not to cross-examine Mr. Dewars at this time, but would very much like to reserve my privilege to recall him later, should that prove necessary."

The judge, always wishing to be solicitous of any course to justice, inquired, "Mr. Cratchit, whom do you wish to interrogate now if not Mr. Hiram Dewars?"

Tim replied, addressing himself to Mr. Dickerson, "Bailiff, please call as the next witness the right honorable and most distinguished Professor Blight."

This proposal prompted quite a hubbub in the courtroom. The cumulated whispers of the spectators gathered in a rolling mass, gushing from the wooden balustrade in front of the gallery to the immense windows just beyond the judge's bench and back again in a tidal wave, crashing upon the ears of the deafest spectator. Calling the prosecutor himself was as unprecedented as it was baffling.

"Professor Blight, I have believed until this very moment that we were strangers in life. Is that so?" asked Tim.

"Yes, I believe it is, for I surely would have recalled meeting so distinguished a barrister as you were, sir. No, I dare say we did not encounter one another in life."

"And yet, sir, I now believe that we each played a central role in the life of Ebenezer Scrooge, and that by the parts we played we were kindred spirits. Would you say that is so?"

Blight appeared troubled and reflective. Befuddlement characterized the looks and thoughts of the gallery as Professor Blight contemplated a truthful but artful reply.

"I cannot say what is meant by kindred spirits. We were fellow travelers to the grave, and in that we all were kindred spirits."

"Professor, you obfuscate. I ask you now directly, did you know Ebenezer Scrooge in life?"

Sweat beaded on the professor's brow. After a long pause and a deep, hissing breath, he replied, "I did."

"And what, Professor, did Mr. Dewars mean when he said to you, 'as I am sure you yourself well remember'?"

"As a barrister concerned with the proprieties of the law, I feel I must not answer your question. It is not for me to judge another's meaning. This is the task of our judge, whose understanding of the facts presented I am sure will suffice to render a rightful decision in this case," answered the professor.

"Your respect for the law is greatly admired by all, Professor, but I, too, have a solemn duty to the law, and I will not be deflected from my course by clever ruses. Tell the court, Professor Blight— did you know both Mr. Scrooge and Mr. Dewars in life?" retorted Tim Cratchit.

"Yes, both. I knew them both."

"And what was your association with Mr. Dewars?"

"We were business associates, as I was with many others, Mr. Scrooge included."

"Did you meet frequently with Mr. Dewars?" inquired Tiny Tim.

"I did, sir, daily, during lunch at our club or for a pint at the George and Vulture."

"And was this not the very club to which Scrooge belonged, and to which the Ghost of Christmas Yet to Come had taken Scrooge in his famed night of ghostly visits?"

"Yes, quite right, sir, though I hardly see how this pertains to the matter currently under consideration."

"It will be clear to all soon enough, Professor. Would you be so kind as to tell the court what facial characteristic of yours you believe to be most noteworthy to others?"

"Alas, my nose is somewhat unusual for the growth that hangs from it, though again, I protest that my anatomy is utterly irrelevant to this proceeding."

"No, Professor, it is not irrelevant at all. Perhaps your memory needs some small assistance. Tell us—here let me hand you a copy of Mr. Dickens's *A Christmas Carol*—to whom was Mr. Dewars speaking when he observed that Scrooge was likely to have a very cheap funeral? Read, if you will, the response from Dickens's own text."

" 'I don't mind going if a lunch is provided,' observed the gentleman with the excrescence on his nose," read Professor Blight in a greatly hurried voice, his eyes, his head—indeed, his entire demeanor—cast down as if he would burrow under the ground.

"Now, Professor, please inform the court whether you and the gentleman with the excrescence on his nose are one and the same."

"One and the same, Mr. Cratchit. One and the same!" admitted a most reluctant Professor Blight, now looking Tiny Tim squarely in the eyes.

Scrooge, leaning forward in his chair, was most engrossed in Tim's line of attack. His eyes, visible to all who might look his way, were placid and passive, but his fingers, barely visible in the shadows cast by the dock, worked feverishly in crushing and disposing of hard raisins as he gazed at Blight. One after another raisin fell silently to the courtroom floor. As each fell, Scrooge murmured Blight's name to himself. Scrooge was happy indeed.

"Then, Professor Blight, we can conclude unequivocally that you were acquainted with Mr. Scrooge in life and that you and Hiram Dewars discussed his character and well-being at the time of his death?" "Yes, we did. What of it? I have already acknowledged that I knew Mr. Scrooge in life because of common business dealings with him."

"Tell us then, kind sir, what opinion did you have of Scrooge's character?" asked Tiny Tim, rising to great stature in the eyes of the gallery, a gallery shocked to learn that the prosecutor himself had intimate ties to the defendant.

"Not much different from Mr. Dewars's, I must say. We both knew Scrooge well, and I shared his views completely."

"Completely, Professor? I am surprised to hear you say that. Mr. Dewars has told us that Ebenezer Scrooge was a cold, calculating man of business with little feeling as we commonly understand that term. Was that your view, too?"

The professor repeated that he shared Dewars's view and noted that, even on learning of Scrooge's death, he was not terribly distraught but rather tied his attendance at the funeral to the prospect of receiving a free lunch.

"Aha," exclaimed Tiny Tim, "but then you must not have shared Hiram Dewars's opinion of Ebenezer Scrooge."

The court seemed quite confused by this exclamation. What did lunch have to do with the salvation or damnation of Scrooge's soul?

"Professor, thank you for your great cooperation," said Tim. "You may step down now. I wish to exercise my right to recall Hiram Dewars."

Blight retreated from the witness's box. Dewars, who had missed all of the aforementioned intercourse because he was in the witness's antechamber, was recalled. Tim Cratchit handed Dickens's book to Dewars just as he had handed it to Professor Blight.

"Mr. Dewars, tell this court again your opinion of Ebenezer Scrooge," said Tim, his eyes twinkling playfully and his chin once again resting comfortably on the cushioned top of his crutch.

"He was a greedy, grasping, coldhearted, bloodsucking man. In short, a monstrous imitation of humankind," responded Dewars.

"Let me remind you, sir, that this tribunal has promised forgiveness to all who may have previously misled the court in making its judgments about Ebenezer Scrooge, provided that they are now truthful. None should feel the slightest hesitation in being candid. No harm may come from speaking freely and honestly in this court. I ask you again, what was your opinion of Ebenezer Scrooge?"

Dewars now wiped his brow, much as Professor Blight had done. He ran his thumb and index finger down the corners of his mouth, drawing his naturally jovial face into a frown—a frown that would last throughout the remainder of his testimony. His voice quivering, he replied, "I do not understand your line of inquiry, sir. I believe I have answered your question satisfactorily twice already."

"Mr. Dewars, I ask you to turn to the fourth chapter of *A Christmas Carol.* Do you deny being the character described by Charles Dickens in that very chapter as the man with the large chin?"

Dewars glanced over to the author, who sat in his accustomed corner, removed from the riffraff in the remainder of the gallery, seeking, perhaps, a nod or signal as to how to proceed, but none was forthcoming. "Yes, that is correct, Mr. Cratchit. The character is me, and I have already quoted from my former self to the effect that we must expect a cheap funeral to which, perhaps, no one would go."

"Yes, so you did. And we are surely to take your words as truthful reflections, isn't that so, Mr. Dewars?"

"Of course, Mr. Cratchit. I would be a fool to speak falsely here, and I pride myself on being no fool."

"Be that as it may, good sir. Allow me now to seek your indulgence. Please turn to *A Christmas Carol* and read aloud to the court from the portion I will instruct you to examine."

"Quite ready, Mr. Cratchit." As Dewars expressed his preparedness in the calmest and most confident of voices, one could easily have thought he had not a care in the world. But his flushed complexion, beaded forehead, and frowning mouth gave the lie to his otherwise composed exterior.

Tim Cratchit pointed to a passage and Hiram Dewars—clearing his throat, sipping from a glass of water, and clearing his throat again—began to read: "'Well, I am the most disinterested among you, after all,' said the first speaker, 'for I never wear black gloves, and I never eat lunch. But I'll offer to go, if anybody else will. When I come to think of it, I'm not at all sure that I wasn't his most particular friend.'"

At these words Tiny Tim slowly lifted his chin from his crutch, flexed his eyebrows so that they curved downward over his eyes, pursed his lips to a rapier point, and raised his left, outstretched index finger into the silent air, signaling Hiram Dewars to cease his recitation.

"What does it mean to say that you never wear black gloves, Mr. Dewars?"

"Well, sir, in that time it was the custom to dispense black gloves to all who attended a funeral. I had no use for such gloves, as I never would have worn them."

"And, of course, it was also the custom to serve lunch to the bereaved, is that not so, Mr. Dewars?"

"Quite so, sir. Quite so. But you see I was not one for lunch or for gloves in those days."

"Mr. Dewars, am I to understand that you had no *utilitarian* purpose in attending Mr. Scrooge's funeral?"

"I guess you are right in that. No utilitarian purpose."

"None at all, Mr. Dewars? No gloves, no lunch, no gain whatsoever? And yet you were prepared to attend. You, a man of business living in a most utilitarian age! Prepared to attend the funeral of a most utilitarian man. Most interesting, Mr. Dewars. Most extraordinary."

Barrister Cratchit, now leaning more heavily than before upon his crutch, pulled himself to his full, yet diminutive, height and spoke: "Your Lordship, it is clear why Mr. Hiram Dewars agreed to attend Ebenezer Scrooge's funeral. He told us straightforwardly himself, in his own—or rather in Mr. Dickens's own—words. Recall the statement of Mr. Dewars: 'I'm not at all sure that I wasn't his most particular friend.' " Tiny Tim directed these words to the judge, but his eyes were cast heavily on Charles Dickens. Tim Cratchit then went on, "What does this phrase—*most particular friend*—mean? How can a man who, according to his creator, was a covetous old sinner, hard as flint, a man without friend or loved one in the world, have at the same time a *most particular friend?* Most particular, indeed! There must, then, have been at least one ordinary friend and at least one particular friend. Perhaps one *more* particular friend before we attain the cardinality of his *most particular friend.* Extraordinary. What is more, we have met some of these friends already in this courtroom. Old Ali Baba certainly counted himself among Scrooge's friends. The Ghost of Christmas Past assured us that Scrooge had friends as a schoolboy. Remember how he looked at Scrooge's lonely childhood school and observed that 'The school is not quite deserted. . . . A solitary child, neglected by his friends, is left there still.' "

Tim Cratchit, who counted himself among Scrooge's friends, proceeded to enumerate those companions as best he could. He did not forget Dick Wilkins, who had himself testified to his deep friendship for Scrooge. Nor Nephew Fred, who also had been a friend. And Jacob Marley! No one must be permitted to ignore the close friendship that Marley and Scrooge shared. Perhaps in the annals of history there has been no closer friendship. Certainly in our age friends have not remained so loyal, even beyond the grave, as did Ebenezer Scrooge and Jacob Marley.

Did not Scrooge say of Jacob, "You were always a good friend to me"? Did not Marley, in an extraordinary show of attachment, tell Scrooge that even after death, "I have sat invisible beside you many and many a day"? Indeed, Jacob Marley returned from the grave for the sole purpose of aiding his old friend Ebenezer, a purpose from which Marley could hope for no personal gain. And oh how Ebenezer had returned Marley's fellowship! Dead seven years, but still Marley's name was firmly affixed to the business establishment they had both helped build. Dead seven years, but still Scrooge answered as readily to Marley's name as to his own. Even Charles Dickens, despite his efforts to mask Scrooge's many close friendships, had to admit that Jacob and Ebenezer were as close a pair of comrades as one could ever hope to see. "They had been," as Mr. Dickens had declared, "two kindred spirits." As had Dewars and Blight and Scrooge been. Kindred spirits in life, yet foes after death.

Tim Cratchit had concluded with Hiram Dewars, but not with Professor Blight or with the court. He turned now to the Judge of All and said, "The prosecutor, a close friend and confidant of Hiram Dewars and admittedly well acquainted with Ebenezer Scrooge in life, is evidently guilty of the subornation of perjury before this tribunal. He has promoted the view that Mr. Scrooge was so uncaring of his fellow beings that he was friendless in life. He has called him a 'friendless, fiendish, insufferable beast.' That claim is a lie, and Professor Blight has known so from the outset. Indeed, if he himself was not Scrooge's friend, he most obviously knew that Hiram Dewars was. Mr. Dewars declared as much directly to Professor Blight, as we have heard at first hand. When the chief prosecutor hides his personal involvement with the defendant and presents perjured testimony as truth, this court cannot possibly take seriously his claims and charges. I demand his dismissal and the dismissal of all charges brought against my client. Mr. Scrooge has been denied a fair hearing and is entitled by law and decency to be admitted to Heaven without delay."

Professor Blight, dejected—even devastated—by the revelations brought forward by Tim Cratchit, nevertheless rallied to present an alternative perspective on what had just transpired.

"I was a man known in life for his pranks, Your Lordship, but never a man who dealt dishonestly or unfairly with the welfare of others. I was a man never afraid of his fellows. I am afraid now, because my deeds and ties to Ebenezer Scrooge have been uncovered but not my motive. You must understand the fear I felt at the hand of Charles Dickens. He possessed the power, with but a stroke of his pen, to end my existence forever. And so it was that I feared in those days more for my own existence than I cared for Scrooge's soul.

"In life, Charles Dickens threatened to cut me off if I wandered beyond his moneymaking course. I could not—I dared not—defy his wishes, and so I willingly participated in my assigned role. My mission was to damage Scrooge's reputation in life and in death, and I pursued that mission with alacrity. Never—you must believe this, Your Lordship—never did I think that Scrooge would suffer particularly on our account.

"His funeral was solitary, it is true, but I thought this was, in a sense, a kindness to him. Seeing how base we could be at his death, I believed he would be excused a little more quickly for his own frailties—frailties that were most prodigious. We were, perhaps, no better than he. It was good for business to be friends with Scrooge, and we were all good men of business. We liked his companionship, but we understood full well his sinfulness and perhaps our own. Our conviction then, as now, was that Scrooge was exactly as Mr. Dickens charged: hard as flint, solitary as an oyster. He was not a good man; he was not a caring man; he was not a compassionate man. I hold these beliefs firmly still.

"It is my fervent wish that the court will indulge me to continue as the prosecutorial voice of this hearing and allow me to strive for the condemnation of Scrooge's soul that has always seemed to me to be the only right and just outcome of this trial. I have never intended to deceive that Judge of All who surely could never be deceived. And I have borne no malice in not revealing my knowledge of Scrooge in life. It seemed to me an irrelevancy. That Mr. Tim Cratchit has seen fit to introduce these facts into this hearing is only a device to deflect the court's attention from the true grievances against this man Scrooge."

Blight continued, "Perhaps my prior acquaintance with Mr. Scrooge was worthy of mention. I cannot be sure. That he was not friendless is a fact I freely admit, a fact I should not have tried to hide, but that I have suborned perjury is a false charge. Your Honor, I have only referred to Scrooge's friendlessness rhetorically in my opening statement. No such charge has been leveled by me or by any witness I have called. No one speaking under oath on behalf of the prosecution has ever emphasized Scrooge's absence of friends as a failing in the man worthy of his eternal damnation. Friendlessness is itself no crime. The accusation against Scrooge is that he was a cold, tightfisted, hard, cruel miser. His other base characteristics are not the issues in dispute. No perjury, then, has been committed or suborned. Therefore, my worthy opponent speaks out inappropriately and in disrespect of this court in declaring that a fair hearing cannot be had and a dismissal is warranted. No dismissal is warranted when the charges are so grave and the evidence so strong against the sinner. I beg the court's indulgence to excuse my excessive enthusiasm in hiding minor facts about my acquaintance with Mr. Scrooge. I beg to be permitted to proceed with these hearings fairly and with minimal threat to my own well-being. That is all that I have ever wished in this matter. That wish remains unaltered, my lord."

CHAPTER FOUR

E VENING fell upon the court like a pall on its past judgments. All went home to rest and prepare for what promised to be a most revealing session. Tim Cratchit had shaken confidence in Professor Blight and in the charge that Ebenezer Scrooge had been friendless in life. But he had not shaken Blight's reputation enough to have him dismissed. The Judge of All chastised Blight but agreed that he would continue as the prosecutor.

In the antechamber of the court, as a crowd of spectators looked on, Dewars, with his eyes downcast and his shame tangible, approached Scrooge. At the end of the day's session, he had at last admitted his long friendship with Ebenezer Scrooge. Now he wanted to make amends for having hidden the truth these past hundred years and more. So great had been his own fear of Dickens, so great had been the fear of so many, that Dewars had hidden behind a vale of lies and misrepresentation even after he passed beyond the grave.

With many gathered around, listening in on Scrooge and Dewars, old Hiram began to speak in a not-too-quiet whisper.

"Ebenezer, forgive me! You know that you always stood well in my esteem, dear friend, for you surely were my most particular friend. Can we not be such friends again?"

"Of course, Hiram, we can be friends again, but only if this court restores my soul to its rightful place and permits your soul to remain where it currently resides or if we both stand condemned. Otherwise, well—we'd best not think of that."

At the thought of condemnation, Hiram shook his head from side to side as if to brush the very thought away. Scrooge continued: "You have wronged me, and this cuts deeply. But I understand fear. Did I not fear the ghosts of Christmas Past, Present, and Future, whose visitations have made my circumstances so well known? Did I not bend to their will as you bent to that of our creator? Can I excuse myself without excusing you? No, Hiram, we can be friends. We must be friends if any good is to come of this. We must be as before, lunch or no lunch," replied Scrooge, and he chuckled at the thought of fat old Hiram abstaining from lunch out of some false illusion that his corporeal being would have less corpus. And oh how foolish that was now, when there was nothing corporeal left for either of them.

This image of corpulent Hiram eschewing lunch accompanied Scrooge quite pleasantly on his journey back to his cold hovel. It seemed almost to warm him against the frost within himself. After walking through several snow-clogged, narrow lanes, Scrooge kicked the slushy trickle in the gutter quite joyously, splashing the filthy runoff all about and chuckling aloud. He arrived shortly at his residence in a particularly good humor.

Eppie welcomed Scrooge at the door and, shivering, took his coat. Scrooge, she observed, did not shiver at all. No cold did he feel; no reddened nose from Jack Frost's bite was upon his face; no chill penetrated to his bone. For a moment—one brief, tiny moment—Eppie wondered how keeping Scrooge's rooms cold could be a punishment for one who seemed so much colder within himself. This thought, however, was gone almost before it was formed. Eppie hung Scrooge's coat behind the door on the hook that had been placed there especially for it. Before yielding up his coat, Scrooge withdrew a small package wrapped in newspaper from its side pocket. "Eppie," said Scrooge, "come, join me in a bowl of porridge. I've brought some honey and raisins to sweeten yours." He smiled at little Eppie as he spoke, and she returned the smile most graciously.

"Oh no, Uncle, I mustn't do any such thing at all. Dear, dear Uncle, how quickly you forget my duty. And your duty, Uncle Ebenezer—we mustn't forget that either. You know there cannot be any hot porridge for you, and we daren't have only cold porridge for me. Oh no, no, that certainly would be most miserable." Eppie said this making the most pouting of faces. Her disconsolate look would have broken the hardest of hearts had she not just then given Ebenezer such a broad and wonderful smile that it pleased him as much—no, more—than if it were a trinket that had cost a fortune.

Eppie, bubbling with excitement as she spoke with her uncle Ebenezer, declared, "What a fine day this has been, Uncle. Oh how much I enjoy the raisins you bring me. Yesterday's were especially wonderful. I let them soak up rum and honey all night long, just the way you showed me, and oh how plump and juicy they were today." She smacked her lips in honor of their memory and rolled her tongue across every rosy corner of her mouth.

Eppie glanced, then, out the window at the dark and snowy scene just beyond the cottage door. Her look was very distant indeed, as if she were trying to see far beyond the confines of their little corner of eternity. After a moment she turned back to Scrooge. "Uncle Ebenezer, will there be time to read tonight?" Before Scrooge could respond, Eppie, on tippy-tippy toes, reached for the old book and took it down from its shelf. As she pushed the volume toward him, she said, "Please say yes! Please, please! It's such fun to hear the funny words and meet the funny characters in your book. I do love it so! Oh please, Uncle Ebenezer, read to me again tonight!"

Eppie continued in this way to implore Scrooge to read to her. None of the troubled foreboding that had lingered with her from the previous night seemed to have survived the day's interlude. None of the fear aroused by her mother's visit could be detected. Eppie was as ebullient and joyous as ever. She showed no care for herself or for the fate that must befall her should Scrooge's petition to enter Heaven fail. No thought did she give to an eternity in hell as the price for her promise to help Scrooge. Quite the contrary, her angelic manner all but insured that Ebenezer would himself forget any dread he felt for his own welfare for the moment. In her happiness she uplifted Scrooge and thawed a little the ice that was within him.

"Eppie, my darling little girl, I would not keep you from hearing this wonderful story for anything. We shall read tonight and read

joyously, and we shall start this very instant, my dear; this very instant. Before we dot another *i* or cross another *t* or pop one more
raisin into your mouth, my dear. Yes, indeedy, we will read right
now. What do you say to that?"

Eppie giggled at Scrooge's attempt to be silly. He was not so very
good at it that you would mistake him for a lighthearted spirit, but
he tried all the same, and with great sincerity, and that was surely
to his credit.

Scrooge began reading softly, almost reverently, to little golden
Eppie. It was difficult for her to follow the tale. The vocabulary was
archaic, and the subject did not seem particularly exciting. Yet
Eppie could no more stop listening to the odd book Scrooge had se-
lected for her than Scrooge could look upon her or the story he told
with cold disinterest. She comprehended only that it gave Scrooge
pleasure, and that was enough for her. His eyes sang with joy as he
turned the page. And so he read aloud these lines until a knock at
the door disturbed the reverie of the child and the man:

> How comes it, then, that thou art out of hell?
> Why, this is hell, nor am I out of it.
> Think'st thou that I, who saw the face of God,
> And tasted the eternal joys of Heaven,
> Am not tormented with ten thousand hells,
> In being depriv'd of everlasting bliss?

Scrooge's demeanor changed and his eyes darkened with the rap-
ping at the door.

"That's all, child. Go at once to your room and shut your door
tight. Be sure it is very tight!"

Scrooge caught the harshness in his tone and knew the dread it
instilled in Eppie. Quickly he smiled at the little girl, as if to chase
away her momentary fear. "My dear sweet, close the door tight to
be sure that no cold air drifts into your bedroom. Now be off, my
precious. I have guests to attend to and much business to discuss."

Eppie, with drowsiness already settling itself upon her eyes,
arched her back in a great and yawning stretch, hugged Ebenezer
Scrooge warmly as if to reassure him that he had dismissed her misgivings, and—carrying her beloved Molly Dolly—retired from the

room. She hesitated not at all, though she would have given anything for a little more of the mysterious book and for the warmth that book instilled in Uncle Ebenezer. But Eppie was an obedient child. Scrooge bent and kissed her on the cheek as she hugged him. He looked wistfully at her little feet as Eppie's steps carried her farther and farther away from him. As he watched her departure, his eyes riveted on her fading image, his arm, in a great sweeping gesture, bade his guests—who could not possibly see him through the door—enter. The knock was repeated as Scrooge exclaimed, "Oh come in, come in, gentlemen. Yes, please enter—come in at once and sit down. "

The door opened slowly to the stomping of feet that wished to be freed from the bitter snow. Tiny Tim pulled the boots from his feet with much grimacing and cursing of the cold darkness. His mild meekness seemed to have given way to a cold demon within him. His shrouded companion wore no boots that any man could see and was disturbed not at all by the bitter cold. Though he wore only a filmy shroud, there was nothing to suggest a shiver within this visitor's essence. This night the two earlier visitors had brought a third with them. Hiram Dewars joined the gathering at Scrooge's cottage. He was in quite good humor, even laughing at the snow he shook from his umbrella, which he opened and closed over and over again. Mr. Dewars pulled his scarf and coat away from his bloated body and inhaled the cold atmosphere of Scrooge's abode with a hearty, jolly laugh.

Greetings were shared all around and whispered conversation about the day's triumphs could be caught amid the buzz. Tim presented a flask of brandy, which he shared with Dewars. Scrooge was untroubled by this seeming slight, apparently preferring to preserve the icy chill within himself rather than imbibe the artificial warmth from the flask. It could never substitute for his own feelings or for the warmth of Eppie. The dark shadow, having no visible means of drinking, showed no notice whatsoever of the brandy. No warmth could warm the chill within that specter's breast. Dewars and Tim alone drank and so were warmed. Their good humor seemed to grow in proportion to their swigs at the flask.

This evening's conversation was most animated. Tiny Tim,

looking older and more wizened than before, seemed gleeful at the trap he had sprung on Professor Blight. Hiram Dewars took this in as if it came as no surprise to him. He revealed not the slightest embarrassment at having been caught, as it were, in Tiny Tim's snare. As taken aback as Dewars had seemed just a few hours earlier, so he seemed perfectly at ease with his current situation. Likewise, Scrooge appeared not at all abashed by the harsh words Dewars had used in describing him that very afternoon. True enough, Hiram had made a public gesture of apology to Ebenezer at the courthouse, and yet it seemed as if Scrooge's tolerance claimed an earlier source. Recollecting Tim's boast at their previous night's meeting: "Be assured, I have made all the necessary arrangements. Tomorrow will be quite exciting for all of us, I promise you!" Scrooge understood that Dewars's apology itself was a play within a play.

"Thankee, Hiram. You have made a great difference, a great difference, I can tell you that—a great difference in our struggle. That wretched Blight will be quite diminished in power from now on. Don't you think so, Tim?" inquired Ebenezer.

"He has been brought closer to the state we desire, to be sure. But care must be ceaseless here. As easily as our mission has progressed these past two days, just so easily may we be kept from our purpose by those who fear your presence in Heaven. We must never lose sight of our goal or look with indifference on any setback. Having you infiltrate the byways of Heaven must be our constant focus," was Tim's cautious retort.

"Come now, Tim. Don't be the lawyer all the time. We are doing splendidly. Hiram has been a great help, and I toast him for it."

As Scrooge lifted a pretend goblet to his lips, Tim, in a mood to be agreeable, offered the flask of brandy to Hiram, who took a deep drink in celebration of the triumphant day.

The dark shadow watched over this scene with keen interest. Its one visible appendage never relented in its attentiveness to the exchange, as if it were the baton conducting the conversation. These four figures remained together for several hours, sometimes laughing loudly, often keeping themselves to such a low whisper that Eppie, in the adjoining room, could not have heard a word even if she had not been sound asleep upon her cot. There was an evil aura about them, yet nothing to palpably cast doubt on their sincerity. They might simply have been men celebrating a day of felicitous testimony, or they might have been men trying the purity of Heaven.

Scrooge, with gracious good cheer, escorted his guests to the door and bade them good night. As he saw them out he felt, for the first time, the cold in his bones, and he shivered. Immediately after the shrouded specter, Tim, and Dewars were out of sight, Ebenezer went to Eppie's room. He pushed the tightly shut door open and clutched the sleeping child in his arms. She awoke, startled to discover Ebenezer by her side. He squeezed his darling Eppie and said, "Don't worry yourself, my little one. We will all be happy in Heaven. Everything will be wonderful, you will see."

Eppie, drowsy from interrupted sleep, was stunned by his cold hands and terrified eyes. She saw that they were moist with tears. Scrooge's reassurances frightened her so that she burst into tears herself.

"What is wrong, Uncle? What is it?"

"Nothing, dearest little one. Why would anything be wrong? On the contrary, everything is wonderful. Everything is going to be fine," repeated Scrooge with such an utter lack of conviction that Eppie was scared all the more. She looked at him with love and pity—pity for them both.

Together Ebenezer and Eppie spent the night sitting on the edge of the little girl's cot, each holding the other, each afraid and not knowing exactly why. Nothing more was said. But there was great comfort in their togetherness, comfort that mercifully, gradually, brought them sleep.

❦

After Tim left Scrooge's cottage, he bade good night to his companions and made haste to another part of the town. There he looked forward to a rendezvous with Molly and a renewal of his efforts to control her soul. He arrived at the cottage first. Molly was nowhere to be seen. Tim, irritated by the need to wait, poured a glass of brandy and warmed himself with it and thoughts of his evening past.

Molly arrived out of breath, carrying old newspapers. Tim, quite irritated and thinking that she had stopped for the papers at his expense, said impatiently, "I told you to be here promptly by eleven o'clock so that I would not be kept waiting. There'll be fewer coins tonight, you can count on that. I'll not tolerate any independence from you." Molly began to raise her right hand in anger. Perhaps she wanted to slap Tim, but, reconsidering, she became contrite, pulling off her blouse and wrapping herself around him. As if to mollify him, she whispered sweet nothings in his ear as they each fulfilled their destinies.

As before, when their business was completed Tim prepared to leave in haste. Before going, however, Molly congratulated him on his performance that day and sought his assurance that Scrooge and Eppie would soon enjoy the privileges of Heaven because of Tim's efforts. Tim did not answer. Then she thrust the newspapers in his hands. Taking them without thought, he tossed the bottle of brandy to Molly, who caught it and imbibed as Tim departed. He was well gone when her tears of fear for Eppie, Ebenezer, and herself flowed freely.

The next morning the court reassembled and the bailiff requested the honor of having Mr. Charles Dickens return to the witness box. The great author strode to the box brimming with self-confidence, seemingly unshaken by the previous day's revelations. He was most assuredly still the great theatrical personage that he had been in life, at least according to his own lights.

For his part Tim continued in his efforts, one by one, to discredit those who aligned against the entry of Ebenezer Scrooge into Heaven.

"Tell us, Mr. Dickens, do you consider yourself an honest man?" inquired Tiny Tim. "A man whose word is worthy of belief?"

"Yes, I do. In life I was a man deeply concerned about the welfare of my fellow beings, and I did all I could to advance that welfare. I was an important voice—pardon my pride—in speaking forthrightly of the degradations of my time, and especially of the injustices committed against the children of England. You, Mr. Tiny Tim Cratchit, were a primary focus of that concern and its beneficiary." Even as the great man spoke, he cast his eyes constantly about, first to one corner, then another, seeking out the nods and waves that greeted him from among the spectators in the gallery. His head tilted in gestures of recognition, while his voice reproachfully attacked the questioning of Tiny Tim. Obviously, Mr. Dickens found the court great sport and his fame and seeming importance a source of wondrous pride and distraction.

"Do you judge yourself to have been a man, then, who wrote honestly of his time; whose statements of character are to be believed as candid declarations of what he understood to be the truth?" pursued Tim sharply, calling the witness's attention back to the serious matter before the court.

"Yes, yes, of course," declared Dickens in an exasperated voice.

"Good, sir. I believe so, too! Now then, what are we to conclude you believed about Ebenezer Scrooge? In your earlier testimony you were rather harsh about his character. Yet how did you describe poor Scrooge at his very first introduction to us? Do you recall?" asked Tim.

"No, I do not recollect the exact description. Only that I surely made evident from the outset that Scrooge was vile," said the author with a dismissive wave of his hand.

"Not quite right, sir! Not quite right at all. Our introduction to Scrooge is most informative, indeed. You, a man who professes to have written honestly about his time, wrote, and I quote, sir, your own words from *A Christmas Carol*, 'Scrooge's name was good upon 'Change, for anything he chose to put his hand to.' Can we fairly interpret that to mean that you, Mr. Dickens, wished us to know that Scrooge was an honest man, trusted by even those most avaricious of men who pursue business as their career; those very men at the Stock Exchange who would have had the least charitable outlook toward a competitor such as Scrooge?"

"I meant to convey that even Scrooge was not without some redeeming quality, but that does not detract one whit from his cold and ruthless ways, Mr. Cratchit. Honest is not kind! Honest is not caring. There are those who can do the proper thing with such an ill will as to make of it a most unpleasant experience. Scrooge was such a man, and he should be condemned for it!"

"And yourself, Mr. Dickens, do you recall what kind of man you said you were? Do you recollect how you described yourself?"

Seeing that Dickens did not recollect or was too embarrassed to recite his own depiction, Tim did so for him: "You wrote of yourself in *A Christmas Carol* that you were *unhallowed*, Mr. Dickens. This, I submit, is a most serious claim. Either we are to dismiss this self-portrait of unholiness as literary license and mere metaphor or we are to take this statement quite to heart. In the first instance, if it was literary license, I do not see how we are to take as faithful testimony *any* of the metaphorical poppycock you have written. Why should we take your charges against Ebenezer Scrooge seriously if we are not to take seriously that with which you have charged yourself! Or in the latter case, if your writing is not mere metaphorical poppycock, we must dismiss your charges against Scrooge as the unholy ravings of a soul that by your own confession is unhallowed."

Blight rose in fury. "Mr. Cratchit—really, sir, I can tolerate no more! First you falsely accuse me of heinous crimes against this court. Now you would slander Mr. Dickens, making wild and altogether contrived accusations against this revered and distinguished gentleman, an artist who engaged in modest metaphor in depicting himself. Have you no shame?"

Tim responded zealously: "Learned professor, you surely know better than I do Mr. Dickens's well-deserved reputation for his careful use of language. It is you who contrive a foolish defense in suggesting that his use of the appellation *unhallowed* is mere modesty on the artist's part. No, Professor Blight and learned judge, Mr. Dickens did not have metaphor in mind. Allow me to prove this with irrefutable evidence from elsewhere in his famed corpus of writing. Mr. Dickens, step aside but stay to hear the testimony of Mr. Charles Darnay." Tim, turning to the gallery, explained that Darnay was the dutiful, devoted, and most revered and honest hero in Dickens's *Tale of Two Cities.*

Charles Darnay approached the bench, nodding graciously to Mr. Dickens, who stepped down. This handsome gentleman, wearing an elegant grey coat topped by a splendid, ruffled collar, took the oath and addressed the court. His wavy head of hair flowed like a great river, cascading over his forehead as the witness bobbed and tucked his head to give emphasis to his words.

"Never did I dream of testifying against Mr. Dickens, yet here I am, Your Lordship, because I know that Mr. Dickens could never speak casually on the subject of being hallowed. The voice he gave me for the ages, and I bless his soul for it, is one of fidelity, integrity, and sincerity. I can no sooner speak falsely for anyone's sake—even my own—than I can escape eternity and return to mortal form."

Darnay continued, "I have known in my time a saintly figure whose suffering and forbearance have touched the hearts of countless souls. I speak, of course, of Dr. Manette, with whom I became acquainted during the terrible days of the French Revolution. I met him thanks to the gracious writing of Mr. Dickens, who created not only me but the fine doctor as well. It was this great author's hand and pen that allowed me to describe Dr. Manette as a man who carried a *hallowed* light about him."

"So what is that to us, Darnay? We are not here to discuss Dr. Manette. I grant you that *he* was a fine gentleman. Be done with it, Darnay," urged Blight.

"But you see, good sir, I could not have uttered such as this unless it were true and sincere. To do otherwise would have contradicted the character given to me by Mr. Dickens. So you see, most honored and esteemed lord, it is my fateful duty to report that here Mr. Dickens spoke of a hallowed soul in great earnest. He could not possibly have chosen this sacred word as a mere trifling, but rather as the sincerest expression of his true meaning, for no less could ever befall Dr. Manette. If ever he used that word casually, then forever must we be uncertain of Dr. Manette's goodness. Such an uncertainty can never be and can never have been our beloved author's true intent."

"Thank you, Mr. Darnay. You have done here today a far, far better thing than you can ever imagine. I thank you, sir, and Mr. Scrooge thanks you from the bottom of his heart," concluded Tiny Tim.

Scrooge declared, "I do, sir, I do indeed!" with such a shake and rattle of his chains that Saint Dunstan, snoring in the gallery, lurched back into wakefulness.

Tim now positively beamed at Blight and Dickens. The latter, betrayed by a soul he had established in honesty and forthrightness for eternity, fuming with anger, turned so red and fiery that Milton's ghost was shocked into sight. Dickens hissed insults at Tim and threatened the entire court with damnation, with fire and brimstone. His face contorted until his lips pulled wide apart and his teeth, like a thousand daggers, took aim at the soul of Ebenezer Scrooge. So deep within himself did his hatred reach that his breath was filled with a repellent, sulphurous, foul smell that engulfed his entire body. The ghost of Charles Dickens then verily flew from the courtroom, Professor Blight running at his tail. Through all of Dickens's histrionics, he did not utter one single word of defense against the charge that *he* was unhallowed. This even he could not do in the presence of the Judge of All.

⊱✦⊰

Tiny Tim's triumphant defeat of Charles Dickens made Scrooge smile without, but within he felt once again the cold shivers and indescribable fear of the previous night. After much shaking of hands among his supporters, Scrooge bade the court farewell for the brief respite afforded by the temporary adjournment brought about by Dickens's disruption of the court.

Bent double, exhausted, like an old rag blown by the wind, Scrooge wandered aimlessly, unthinkingly, from the courthouse. Tilting against the buffeting snow, his body bore a tortured expression while his face preserved the false smile he had shown his supporters. What thoughts might be conveyed within his soul at that moment no one could have guessed. But on he walked, with a determination to wear away the hours before his trial reconvened and to wear well the recollection of Dickens's fall.

After some time of walking in this way, Scrooge became aware that the decaying cottages surrounding him were the familiar abodes of his neighborhood. He noticed smoke rising from the chimney of a nearby shop and, attracted to the smoke's ascent above the snow, paused to look inside. It was the very shop from which he had purchased raisins that morning and every morning since his arrival. Slowly pulling the gloves from his hands, finger by deliberate finger, Scrooge entered the fruiterers.

"Mr. Scrooooge, is it?" inquired the shopkeeper. "What's you doin' here at this toim of day, sir? I should 'ave thought you'd be quoit toid up, as it were, sir, in court an' all at least 'til the sun 'ere would 'ave set for the noit."

Scrooge, emerging from his inner thoughts and becoming sensible that he was in the company of the shopkeeper, Mr. McGreasy, offered a gentle but not especially warm smile.

"There's been a brief respite, my dear fellow, a momentary interlude. I've taken advantage of it to take a little walk, to enjoy the fine weather hereabouts, and to think," responded Scrooge.

"Foin weatha' indeed, sir. This 'ere snow ain't never goin' to stop if'n you ask me."

The gentleman behind the counter seemed quite content to pursue the subject of the weather once Scrooge had mentioned it. And why not? His shop was warm and tight against the bleak outdoors, and so was he. His thinning white hair was covered by a little blue cap, and he wore an apron over his tattered but warm coat. He had an adequate fire blazing on the grate in one corner.

As he spoke with Scrooge, Mr. McGreasy was carefully arranging the display of fruits in his shop. He seemed especially attentive to the basket of oranges he kept on the edge of the counter. Scrooge took particular notice of those fruits and of the gentleman's care for them.

"Lovely oranges you have there," commented Ebenezer, feeling quite in the mood to entertain this chap with a bit of talk and, perhaps, even gossip.

"Oh yes, sir—they are, sir. These 'ere beauties are a golden treasure, I can tell you that. There ain't many in this neighborhood what's ever 'ad enough money to boi one of these, sir. Oh no—mark me word—they're dear indeed. But you, sir, you never boi none of them noither. Just me raisins, ain't that so, sir?"

"Yes, Mr. McGreasy, it is. And I tell you what—I'll take a small bundle of raisins just now if it pleases you."

"Quoit, sir. Only be tellin' me which ones'll it be, sir—the 'ard ones what you boi most mornins on your way to court or the soft and juicy ones what you boi most noights on your way back to that darlin' little girl what I 'ear so much about? Eppie—ain't that 'er name then, Mr. Scrooooge?" inquired McGreasy.

Scrooge, caught up in McGreasy's observation of his raisin-buying habits, did not notice his mention of Eppie at all. Perhaps he had not noticed this pattern of behavior in himself: hard raisins by day—hard for himself, hardness for the hardness within him; soft raisins by night—soft for Eppie, soft for the softness within her. As he thought about the raisins, his mind drifted to reflections on Eppie. And this made Scrooge begin to thaw a little inside. Alas, as he warmed to his conversation with the fruiterer, McGreasy interrupted his thoughts:

"Seein' as 'ow it's the afternoon just now, Mr. Scrooooge, I'm 'ard pressed to know just what it is your wantin' from me—'ard raisins or soft ones?"

Scrooge smiled coldly at Mr. McGreasy. "Give me a small sack of hard ones. They'll suit my purpose just perfectly, sir," replied Scrooge with an air of mystery. He placed a few pennies on the bare counter. Scrooge then carelessly picked up one orange, tossed it gently in the air, and caught it back in his hand while the fruiterer looked on with consternation.

"You'll not want to be 'andlin' those beauties, Mr. Scrooooge, unless you're wantin' to boi one, and they are moity dear, sir, if you take me meanin', moity dear indeed, Mr. Scrooooge."

Ebenezer gave McGreasy a hard look and, smiling the whole time, continued to chat amiably about this and that while he took a handful of money from his pocket. Scrooge, his eyes glistening youthfully, smacked the coins on the counter. McGreasy smiled, revealing the great cavity in his mouth where two front teeth ought to have been. The money was ample to purchase the orange with which Ebenezer was toying. Now, having become its owner, Scrooge tossed the fruit high in the air and, with McGreasy looking on in absolute astonishment, walked away while it fell to the floor, splattering with a thwat.

"Orange juice for you, McGreasy," called Scrooge as he shut the shop door behind him. He laughed loudly at this without ever turning back to see McGreasy's shocked look.

Now, once again tilting against the snow's forceful descent but no longer shivering, Scrooge trudged on toward the courthouse. The way took him by a broad field of virgin snow. With a great smile, he tossed his head back as he marched through the field, destroying its virginity by tossing hard raisins high in the air and listening for the sound made by those he did not catch in his open mouth.

⟨❦⟩

A few minutes more were all the walk that was required to transport Scrooge back to the scene of his trial. He spent these minutes in solitary pleasure, reflecting with renewed vigor and confidence on the positive turn of events that had ended the day's previous session. Whatever earlier fear had grasped Ebenezer seemed to have retired from his thoughts. Dickens and Blight were indisputably in disarray. With these happy thoughts commanding his attention, Scrooge arrived just as the court reconvened.

The entire atmosphere of the tribunal seemed changed by the morning's events. Even the oak arches of the courtroom and its high, vaulted ceiling appeared taller, stronger, more stately. Professor Blight, damaged by the charges leveled against him and against his star witness, was eager to get on with the business of Scrooge's condemnation. He immediately called the next witness: Joe the Pawnbroker.

Joe was a stubby fellow, mangy in appearance but mannerly in an oddly formal way. The pawnbroker's whiskers had the cultivated unkemptness of a man who had maintained a five-day-old stubble all his adult life. He had operated a seedy business, a rag-and-bottle shop, buying and selling any used thing that came his way. No object was too mean to be of interest to Old Joe, and no price was too low for him to be embarrassed by offering it. To buyers, be assured, Joe extolled the virtues of every good, from fragments of bright calico to deathbed linens; from solid door hinges to the iron mongery of a casket. Old Joe had been a poor and dishonest man of business during Scrooge's later years, but he had not been unkind as unkindness went in his trade. He was not despised for his dishonesty but rather respected as a fair-minded dealer in trade. Indeed, Joe was a good man. He provided a service and an opportunity for the lowly among London's society. Without such men as he, who knows how many poor, bereaved servants might have found their way to the poorhouse? Instead, they turned to Joe to buy the remains their employers had abandoned in death. Joe stayed the hand of starvation by the payments he made for his purchases and thought himself nearly saintly for doing so.

Old Joe had truly been old when he came to know Ebenezer Scrooge, or rather when Ebenezer Scrooge's remains came to know Old Joe. Not, of course, his bodily remains. Those Joe never saw in life—nor, in fact, had he seen them even now. His vision had long been clouded by the constant immersion of his eyes in smoke. Joe was an inveterate pipe smoker who had died, finally, of emphysema complicated by his habit of imbibing tobacco smoke from his pipe's stem like a babe sucks its mother's milk. But we wander from our course. That Joe had not known Scrooge nor even known of him by name was all to the good according to Professor Blight. At last the court would hear a witness who was not one of the vested interests, a witness merely to the facts of Scrooge's miserliness.

"Does this court have the pleasure of addressing itself to Mr. Joseph Poure?" asked Professor Blight of the witness.

"Most honored to reply that yes it does, sir! Although only me mum ever called me that. If it please Your Honor, I should much rather be known as Old Joe or just as Joe. I don't want to appear at all uppity in the eyes of the court, but I don't want me friends to be goin 'bout callin' me Mr. Poure either," exclaimed Old Joe, smiling through his mostly toothless gums. He was, of course, known as Old Joe from that moment forward.

Professor Blight explained, "Old Joe, you are here merely to answer a few questions about Ebenezer Scrooge. We have no interest in your affairs beyond the light they shed on this man Scrooge. Do not worry yourself one iota, good sir, regarding any wrong dealings in which you, perchance, might from time to time have engaged. These are not at all the subject before the court."

"Thankee, Your Lordship," responded Old Joe as he wiped the greasy offal from his mouth, disposing of it on his dirty suit jacket without the slightest self-consciousness. "You must have the wrong man in me, sir. I could not be the man you want, 'cause I don't know no one named Scrooge and never did. What then can I add to these haughty deliberations, I ask ya?"

"Quite so. We know that you never knew Scrooge, we know that quite fully. Indeed, Mr. Pou—oh, excuse me—Old Joe, everyone in the court realizes that you have never made the acquaintance of Ebenezer Scrooge. That is all to the good sir, to the very good," said the professor.

"I am quite confused then, Your Lordship. If I don't know the man, how can I help inform this court about him?"

"Joe, let me help you help us. Do you recollect a Mrs. Dilber, a laundress in London in the year eighteen hundred and forty-three?" asked Blight.

"The year is somewhat fuzzy, Your Honor. It was a long time ago and I was already quite old by then, but of course I remember Mrs. Dilber. She was a fine woman—handsome, too, for one in her way of life. We did considerable business together, she and me. We was quite a number, we was."

"Joe, I want you to think back to one particular transaction that you had with her. It involved not only Mrs. Dilber but also Mrs. Quillan, a charwoman from Camden town, and Haman Sloth, the undertaker's man. Do you know these people?" inquired the professor.

"Yes, certainly. They were all good, humble people of little means. From time to time each brought an odd lot of this or that to me shop," replied Old Joe. Again he caught the greasy drippings that had escaped his mouth and lathered their way down his chin. This time he flung them on the ground without thinking and was chastised by the court for doing so. Old Joe's spittle, so recently discarded, dribbled in a stream between the old stones of the courtroom floor. It was as an ocean of opportunity for the buzzing flies that were instantly attracted from the stench of the onlookers to this more promising nectar. The judge was quite repulsed by Old Joe's lack of decorum. However forgiving in nature this judge sought to be, still Joe was firmly rebuked for his untoward behavior. Joe—having formed the habit of spitting early in life—continued, with profuse apologies and no malevolent intentions, to expectorate on the cold stones. As he was unable even now, beyond the grave, to undo this habit, the judge had a spittoon brought in to assist Mr. Poure in being more discrete about his indiscretions.

Professor Blight continued his interrogation. "We, sir, are interested in one occasion in particular. Do you recall Mrs. Dilber, Mrs. Quillan, and Mr. Sloth coming to your shop all together, with the belongings of a man recently deceased carried in heavy, tightly wrapped bundles?"

"No, sir, I recollect no such particular meeting. It was common as spit—excuse me language, Your Lordship—for such as them to come to me shop bearing bundles. I would not remember one time in particular over their many visits, sir," responded Old Joe.

"Perhaps I can help you remember. It was a most unusual meeting. Normally, those good enough to frequent your establishment were embarrassed by being seen there. Yet these three were in quite good cheer at one another's presence," noted the learned barrister.

Joe continued to look befuddled.

Blight, sure that the memory would return, went on, "Remember, Mrs. Quillan proposed the order in which they presented their goods, declaring: 'Let the charwoman alone be the first! . . . Let the laundress alone to be the second; and let the undertaker's man alone to be the third. Look here, Old Joe, here's a chance! If we haven't all three met here without meaning it.'"

Although there was nothing obviously special about these words, the witness seemed sparked by recollection. Blight knew just how to take Joe and all the court back to that long-ago encounter.

In Joe's rag-and-bottle shop bits of old clothing and torn fabric, covered with the grit and grime of London life, hang everywhere. On a crate sits Old Joe, his hands wrapped in fingerless gloves, sipping at his pipe, sorting rusted keys, and recording the occasional shilling that finds its way into his hands. Three people, a man and two women, wander into his shop, each toting bundles on their backs. Through all these many years that scene had withdrawn deeply from Joe's consciousness. But now it returned to him as if it had been but yesterday. So vivid was his recollection of every detail that Old Joe veritably thought he had once again become his younger self, still living and breathing the very dusty air of his wretched business establishment.

Joe's apparition turned toward the three customers and, looking at one in particular:

"You couldn't have met in a better place," said Old Joe, removing the pipe from his mouth. "Come into the parlor. You were made free of it long ago, you know; and the other two an't strangers. Stop till I shut the door of the shop. Ah! How it skreeks! There an't such a rusty bit of metal in the place as its own hinges, I believe, and I'm sure there's no such old bones here as mine. Ha, ha! We're all suitable to our calling, we're well matched. Come into the parlor. Come into the parlor."

The old man raked the fire together with an ancient stir rod, and having trimmed his smoky lamp (for it was night) with the stem of his pipe, put it in his mouth again and smiled at his guests.

While he did this, the woman who had already spoken threw her bundle on the floor and sat down in a flaunting manner on a stool, crossing her elbows on her knees and looking with a bold defiance at the other two.

"What odds, then? What odds, Mrs. Dilber?" said the woman. "Every person has a right to take care of themselves. *He* always did!"

"That's true, indeed!" said the laundress. "No man more so."

"Why then, don't stand staring as if you was afraid, woman; who's the wiser? We're not going to pick holes in each other's coats, I suppose?"

"No, indeed," said Mrs. Dilber and the man together. "We should hope not."

"Very well, then!" cried the woman. "That's enough. Who's the worse for the loss of a few things like these? Not a dead man, I suppose."

"No, indeed," said Mrs. Dilber, laughing.

"If he wanted to keep 'em after he was dead, a wicked old screw," pursued the woman, "why wasn't he natural in his lifetime? If he had been, he'd have had somebody to look after him when he was struck with death, instead of lying gasping out his last there, alone by himself."

"It's the truest word that ever was spoke," said Mrs. Dilber. "It's a judgment on him."

"I wish it was a little heavier one," replied the woman; "and it should have been, you may depend upon it, if I could have laid my hands on anything else. Open that bundle, Old Joe, and let me know the value of it. Speak out plain. I'm not afraid to be the first nor afraid for them to see it. We knew pretty well that we were helping ourselves before we met here, I believe. It's no sin. Open the bundle, Joe."

As Joe's long-ago self leaned forward to undo the bundle, the scene returned to Scrooge's trial. Scrooge, sitting in his lonesome corner, trembled at the utter lack of compassion these people felt for his passing. Too well did he recall the scene just played over for the court. In his own lifetime the Ghost of Christmas Yet to Come had allowed him to witness this selfsame exchange at Joe's shop. His trembling gave way to feelings of pride and reassurance as he recollected Eppie and Molly and their warm and loving feelings for him.

Old Joe, dumb struck by the scene that had just been displayed, observed to Professor Blight, "I remember the day, Your Lordship. Oh yes, I remember it well. It is as clear in me mind as if it were this mornin'. But how did you know 'bout it? We was quite discreet, I believe—quite discreet indeed."

"Don't trouble yourself about it, Joe. We want to make no trouble for you here. We just want—now that you remember the visit— for you to be so kind as to enumerate for us the goods brought to you on that occasion."

Joe, quite proud of his ability to remember past business dealings, declared, "As best as I recall, which is mighty good if I say so meself, sir. I had a gift for me calling, you see, and recollection of what was what and whose was whose was the key to success and to not falling on the wrong side of the constable. As best as I recall, then, the ladies and the undertaker's man brought—ah, yes—they brought a seal or two, a pencil case, a pair of sleeve buttons, and a brooch of no great value. Sheets and towels, a little wearing apparel, two old-fashioned silver teaspoons, a pair of sugar tongs, and a few boots . . . bed-curtains . . . his blankets . . . a shirt—the best he had, I believe."

"Would you say that was a great quantity for a rich man?" inquired the professor.

"Not at all, sir—more like the holdings of a poor man or a miser, I should say."

"Did you know many misers in your time, Joe?"

"Oh yes, sir, most assuredly, sir. Not personal, you understand, but more through their remains. Them what hoarded their money, they was first to have their things brung to me shop when they went on to their reward, you can be sure. I should say so, Mr. Blight, yes indeedee. Them what had little out o' malice for spendin' their money, they was not likely to take what little they had to the grave. And right enough that be, for they was more despicable in life than any, if you want my opinion."

"Thank you, Joe. You have been most helpful. Your witness, Mr. Cratchit."

Tim, feeling that Joe could only be trouble for Scrooge's cause, smiled at the old rag-and-bottle man and merely said, "You may step down now."

"That's it, then?" asked Joe, somewhat astonished that his recollections and opinions could be of interest or of use to so high a court. Except for the professor's knowing about the particular encounter in Joe's shop, it all seemed tiresome and inconsequential to him.

As Joe left the stand, Professor Blight looked around the court. The scene before him was quite pleasing. The gallery was enthralled by Joe and his testimony. Blight savored their reaction, allowing the malice of the gallery for Scrooge's ill-used wealth to build to a peak before speaking again. The judge did not interrupt but rather allowed Blight to consume the moment. After a few seconds of silence, Blight reflected to all assembled there on the meaning of Old Joe's testimony.

"Most honored Judge, learned colleagues, what are we to make of Joe's testimony? Here is a simple man, the proprietor in life of a rag-and-bottle shop. A man who knows nothing whatsoever of the business of this court. He is a man who never met Ebenezer Scrooge in life nor even heard his name. He is, by dint of his former occupation, an acknowledged expert on people's affairs. A cloth here, a shoe there, a revealing button are all Old Joe needs to know those who spent their wealth and those who hoarded it. He has told us that Scrooge possessed the goods of a poor man or a miser. Ebenezer Scrooge, avowedly an excellent man of business, possessed the meager objects that better befit a man of lowly station than a man obsessed with money and all its worth. We can only conclude, my learned friends and colleagues, that Scrooge was—as so many have previously testified and as Joe himself suspected—a miser. What else can we possibly make of Scrooge? This man Scrooge was . . ."

Scrooge, with malicious rage in his eyes, jumped to his feet. "Enough of this. At last, enough! How dare you, you slithery toad," he shouted. "I cannot understand a court that will tolerate such drivel from this fool, this contemptible spittle, this outrage who has already admitted to being co-conspirator with Charles Dickens against my very salvation. Throw him out. I demand it. I demand some consideration here, some, some"—being at a loss for words, Scrooge rambled and rattled his chains in defiance of the tribunal and then went on. "What's the use? What care have you for justice? What care have any of you? What do any of you know of suffering or of me? Nothing, all of you understand nothing, nothing at all."

Tiny Tim lunged as best as his lame leg permitted toward Scrooge to reseat him and urge him to silence. Mr. Dickerson ever so much more quickly wrenched Ebenezer back into his seat by grabbing a sturdy link of Scrooge's chain and yanking hard upon it. He need not have done so. Drained of energy, his outpouring of anger completed, Scrooge had become insensible to his surroundings. He was lost in thought about Eppie. He whispered to himself, "My dear little one, I will not let you suffer ever again! Never!" None in the court heard this thought.

The judge instructed the accused in no uncertain terms: "It is hard, no doubt, Mr. Scrooge, to hear such things about oneself. To have been a miser is one of the most damaging charges that can be brought against any person. To have had the wherewithal to help those less fortunate in life and not to have done so is damnable indeed. If this charge withstands the scrutiny of your able attorney,

Mr. Scrooge, your future will be harder still than has been the hearing of these claims. Your turn at defense will come, sir, but only if you sit down and remain silent. This court will not tolerate such behavior. You will not address any witness or any officer of this court with such contempt again if you hold any hope of salvation. Is that understood?"

The thought that his outburst endangered Eppie's soul along with his own had made Scrooge regret his loss of temper even before the judge spoke. Now, returned to his senses and filled with chilling fear, he dared not even respond to the question just put to him. Fortunately, Tiny Tim quickly interjected his and Mr. Scrooge's apologies.

"We are under the greatest strain, Your Lordship. It is only Mr. Scrooge's fear and fatigue speaking. No harm was meant. No such outburst will happen again, I promise you."

Tim offered a similar apology to his learned—and hated—opponent. Professor Blight went on with his speech, energized by his resentment of Scrooge, pointing harshly at the defendant. "This man was the evil miser whose presence iced his office in the dog days and didn't thaw it one degree at Christmas. This mean, pinching, scrimping, scraping spirit kept the coal box in his own room, and so surely as his clerk came in with the shovel, Scrooge predicted that it would be necessary for them to part. Truly, he was a cold affliction on all unlucky enough to have dealings with him. That is the meaning of Old Joe's testimony: Scrooge was a tight-fisted hand at the grindstone. A wealthy, hard, moneylending wretch, he deprived all around him—even himself—of the slightest comfort. Scrooge gave nothing, save a fright, even to the poor children who came to sing a merry Christmas carol at his doorstep. He ate gruel for his Christmas supper and praised the poor laws as if they were charity enough for those who felt want most keenly. His own brief suffering in childhood, his own labors for good after his fateful Christmas visitations, must all be overshadowed by his inner cold and unfeeling miserliness. This is the unforgivable essence of Ebenezer Scrooge, and we have heard it from Old Joe, a disinterested soul who had never even cast his eyes upon the accused. Can any of us doubt his failings any longer? Is it not time to end this tribunal once and for all? Can anyone claim merit enough to overcome the accursedness of this rogue who inspired not one happy thought among all mankind except in the prospect of his passing? No, Scrooge was not an innocent victim; he was an evil man, and he must be condemned." Blight, with a hateful look at his old acquaintance, returned to his seat.

Tim, still perturbed by Scrooge's loss of control, assured the court that he would prove once and for all that Ebenezer Scrooge was not a miser but rather was an altruist, himself deeply impoverished but generous to a fault. Hoots of derision leapt forth from a contingent in the gallery who were outraged by Tim's suggestion. They were swiftly silenced by the Judge of All. Cratchit, undeterred by the gallery's response, called for Mrs. Laura Dilber, the late laundress of Ebenezer Scrooge. Scrooge smiled warmly at the old woman's ghost.

Laura Dilber paid no heed to Scrooge's smile. She was old and exceedingly wrinkled, but she had an honest demeanor. Her hair, though unkempt, was not dirty. Her clothing, though ragged, was clean. Here was truly a laundress who took the responsibilities of her trade quite seriously. Mrs. Dilber had no great liking for Ebenezer Scrooge, but neither did she dislike him. There was between them the distance common among master and servant throughout the ages. He had been her employer, she his employee, and this barrier was too great ever to be traversed in her mind's eye. But she respected Scrooge, and she had known his condition better than most.

At the bailiff's request, Mrs. Dilber placed her right hand upon the Bible and swore, with earnest solemnity, that she would tell the truth, the whole truth, and—most assuredly—nothing but the truth, so help her God. She completed this declamation trembling before the Judge of All and taking the promise's meaning more deeply than she could ever have done before.

"Mrs. Dilber, you have heard testimony today from Old Joe, the pawnbroker. Do you corroborate the testimony in all its particulars?" asked Tiny Tim in a gentle, caring voice.

Mrs. Dilber, put somewhat at ease by Tim's manner, responded quickly but very softly. "Yes, Your Lordship, I do. Joe told of our meeting just the way it was."

"Very good, Mrs. Dilber. And now, could you tell the court whether Professor Blight's summary of Joe's testimony was likewise accurate in all its particulars?" asked Tim.

"Why, no!" said Mrs. Dilber.

"No, you cannot attest to the professor's accuracy, or no, you are unable to tell the court, Mrs. Dilber?"

"No, what the professor said ain't the way it was. Ain't the way it was at all! Sure, Old Scrooge was a grump, but he was no miser— no sir, not he," said Mrs. Dilber.

Professor Blight straightaway objected, declaring, "Mrs. Dilber is drawing a conclusion for which she is not qualified whatsoever."

The judge addressed the witness:

"Dear lady, it is most important, most earnestly important, that you limit your testimony only to those facts about which you, dear Mrs. Dilber, have personal knowledge."

"I am only an ignorant old lady," said Mrs. Dilber, "and not at all accustomed to the ways of this court. I meant no harm, Your Honor."

The judge spoke gently, saying, "None is taken, Laura." A kindly smile from the judge was just enough to restore her composure.

Tim returned to his interrogation of the witness, phrasing his questions more carefully.

"Mrs. Dilber, what do you take the word *miser* to mean?" asked Tim.

"Well, to me it is someone of means what is so cheap that he don't do nothing what is good for anyone with his money. He don't even do to help himself live better than a poor man."

Tim inquired of the court, and most particularly of Professor Blight, as to whether this simple woman's definition of a miser was found suitable and acceptable or whether it suffered some flaw of which the learned professor might be aware. Blight nodded agreeably, indicating that Mrs. Dilber's definition was most pertinent, as it surely was consistent with everything that had been learned of Scrooge's money-grubbing ways.

"Mrs. Dilber, Ebenezer Scrooge stands accused of miserliness.

You have confirmed that he owned almost nothing, gave almost nothing, did almost nothing, thought almost nothing of his fellow beings. We have all heard testimony that he was not so generous as to separate himself from a few shillings at Christmastime for the sake of the poor, the too proud, and the infirm. How, then, can it be that he was not a miser? Is not the description I just recollected for you precisely what you mean by the word miser?" asked Tim.

"Your Lordship makes it seem as there is no way Mr. Scrooge could be anything but a miser. But you ain't speaking right of him, sir. You start from some notion that he had what to give to others that he did not give. Perhaps he was poorer than you think. Perhaps he had not what to give beyond what he was giving. Perhaps he gave and you didn't know it," responded the laundress.

"Come now, Mrs. Dilber. What evidence is there that Scrooge was poorer than is generally thought? He was, as no one has denied, an excellent man of business," said Tim.

Mrs. Dilber, wanting to be well understood, asked Tim if he had made a careful study of the evidence. Not waiting for a response and obviously intending her question to be rhetorical, she reminded Tim—precisely as he had hoped she would—of her very words to Old Joe regarding Ebenezer Scrooge.

"Mr. Cratchit, you of all people here, bein' the defender of Mr. Scrooge an' all, should know that he was not a man of means. He lived as good as he could, which was none too good to be sure. Don't you recall me and Mrs. Quillan saying of Mr. Scrooge: 'Every person has a right to take care of themselves. *He* always did!' 'That's true, indeed! . . . No man more so.'"

Tim Cratchit approached closer to Mrs. Dilber, his eyes agleam.

"Mrs. Dilber, are we to take your testimony to mean that Scrooge lived as well as he could *afford*?"

"Just so, sir—as plain as day. Mr. Scrooge was careful to take good care of himself within his means. He was considerate of his comforts, as is every man's right. He didn't have much, it is true; he never had much, did he? Wasn't he living with only the belongings he inherited from his partner, poor Mr. Marley, having had none to call his own when Mr. Marley, God rest his soul, passed on? And the rooms of his flat was not much, I can tell you that, sir. They was a gloomy suite of rooms, in a lowering pile of building up a yard. It was old enough and dreary enough, for nobody lived in it but Mr. Scrooge. The yard was so dark that even he, who knew its every stone, was fain to grope with his hands. It was an uncommonly miserable place, but it was the best what he could manage, poor Mr. Scrooge. Just like Mr. Marley, he was."

"But Mrs. Dilber, how then could Mr. Scrooge have been a miser? Were we not given to understand that a miser is so cheap that he takes not care even of himself for fear of dissipating his own wealth?" Tim Cratchit asked.

"Like I said, sir, Mr. Scrooge was no miser! That's my whole point. He was poor in money. Not so poor as me or Mrs. Quillan, God knows, but poor enough. I used to snicker in his day at the common folks what whispered that he was a rich man, sir, for I could see for myself that he did as good as he could do. He was no miser. He was fair enough with me and most generous, sir—most generous, indeed—to your own father, as you must surely know."

Professor Blight thought Tim's line of inquiry mere sophistry and as much as said so. "Your Honor, surely we are not to take Mrs. Dilber's contention seriously. She is no authority on wealth and could not possibly know what Scrooge had squirreled away for the proverbial rainy day. She could not know that he was a poor man, a claim which runs contrary to everything else we know of this *excellent man of business.*"

"My lordship," spoke up Tiny Tim, "perhaps we have all mistakenly placed the emphasis on Scrooge's excellence in business rather than on the excellence of the man! However, Professor Blight is correct in one regard. We must not take Mrs. Dilber's word for Mr. Scrooge's poverty or generosity. Rather, we must submit firm and incontrovertible evidence. This I now propose to do."

—— CHAPTER FIVE ——

Eppie, playing with her dolly, heard a tapping on the cottage door. She caught her breath and hid her doll, afraid that some terrible evil might hurt it, then slowly made her way to the door. She whispered to herself, "Maybe this is the visitor Mummy told me about. Oh I hope so."

The shrouded figure stood in the doorway. Eppie started, involuntarily stepping back from the door's threshold, and then thought that she must slam the cottage door shut against the unexpected visitor and its sinister outstretched index finger. And yet some unseen force prevented her from doing so.

"What do *you* want?" Eppie asked boldly, hiding her fear as best she could. And then, softening toward the shrouded apparition, Eppie, went on, "Are you the spirit whose coming was foretold to me?"

"I am!"

The voice was soft and gentle, almost familiar. Singularly low, as if—instead of being so close beside her—it were at a distance.

"Who and what are you?" Eppie demanded.

"I am the Ghost of Christmas Future."

"My future?" inquired Eppie, observant of its fearful finger.

"No, Ebenezer Scrooge's future."

"Oh and are you here from the court? Is the trial over? Is Uncle Scrooge coming home, free?"

The only answer that the specter gave was to beckon Eppie close by its side. To every gesticulation of its finger, she stepped closer.

Standing on her tippy toes, she still could not discern the ghost's intent. The figure bent down and whispered to Eppie, "You must steal into the courtroom today. We have planned on your being there. We need you."

"But why—what am I to do? I'm not supposed to go there, am I?" "You will know what to do when the time comes, child. And child, make sure to remind Tiny Tim about the newspapers. Trust in yourself and you cannot help but trust in me."

"I don't understand. I don't know anything about newspapers. I can't even read."

"You will know what to do and when to do it. Trust in me."

⌘

Tim requested the court's indulgence to permit him to present exhibits demonstrating Scrooge's privation and benevolence. He would resume calling witnesses momentarily, but first certain economic facts must be established.

"My lord, a man who is excellent at business must, to be true to the meaning of excellence, be a man who is successful at earning his wealth and fortune from the dealings of his trade. Scrooge's trade was lending money. This itself is a noble undertaking, much like Old Joe's pawnbrokerage. Both the banker and the pawnbroker provide a means of obtaining cash for those in need of it. Why should we perceive Old Joe to have been generous enough but think Scrooge a money-grubbing, avaricious lout? Yes, Scrooge lent money to those much in need of it, and he lent it most assuredly on easy terms, and so he was a failure in business."

Professor Blight sprang from his seat. "Your Honor, must we hear such outlandish claims? Ebenezer Scrooge was well known for his moneylending ways. He is famed the whole world wide for his ceaseless yearning for gold. He loved it as you might love a child. He lent it to recover its fully grown and matured offspring. He never hesitated in its pursuit no matter how hard his course might be on others. Even Christmas Eve gave no respite to his greed. Surely we can be spared whatever new fallacy my learned opponent has dreamt up to make good what was plainly evil."

The judge, with compassion for Professor Blight's tribulations, said, "We must hear Tiny Tim Cratchit out if we are to judge fairly of all the facts. Nothing is so well known the whole world wide as that nothing is as plain as it may seem. Nothing is so well loved by me—not even a child—as the truth. If Tim is engaged in casuistry, I pray that the professor will expose it more fully than by asserting its presence. For now, we must neither preclude Tiny Tim from making his case nor inhibit Professor Blight from his appointed course. Mr. Cratchit, be so kind as to enlighten this court with the presentation of evidence."

"Ah, evidence!" sighed Tiny Tim. "Let us reflect on the three moneylenders we encountered during Scrooge's tale. Yes, three, my learned colleagues and esteemed judge: Fezziwig, Marley, and Scrooge. Marley and Scrooge we already know were kindred spirits; partners in business; friends in life and even beyond the grave. Marley and Scrooge; Scrooge and Marley—they acted as one, thought as one, lived as one. Scrooge as readily answered to Marley's name as to his very own. Marley and Scrooge—interchangeable beings, equal in life, equally burdened by equally ponderous chains as death approached. Scrooge and Marley! Marley, described in Charles Dickens's own hand as a liberal soul. After all, it was one of Mr. Dickens's own creations who approached Scrooge for a charitable donation, noting that 'we have no doubt Marley's liberality is well represented by his surviving partner.' Once again we must believe Mr. Dickens to have given a truthful voice to his characters, in which case we know that there was *no doubt* of Scrooge's liberality, or we must conclude that Dickens lies at will, making his entire accusation against poor Mr. Scrooge scurrilous and reprehensible, depriving the court of any basis for condemning goodly Ebenezer to hellish damnation.

"Now let us consider Mr. Scrooge in comparison to his former employer, Mr. Fezziwig. Between Marley and Scrooge they had but one employee—my father, Mr. Robert Cratchit. Mr. Fezziwig, by contrast, had no fewer than thirty-two employees in his counting-house, and likely there were more."

"One moment, Mr. Cratchit," interrupted Professor Blight. "Please be so kind as to enlighten us as to how you derived this number thirty-two."

"Please recall, Professor Blight," continued Tim Cratchit, "that Fezziwig's Christmas party, which we briefly witnessed earlier in these proceedings, had four and twenty couples dancing. Let us take this number—twenty-four—times two plus one to be the minimum number of people at the party. Times two because, you see, *couples dancing* means two at a time. Plus one because the fiddler could not possibly have been among the dancers, as he was providing the music to which they performed. Fezziwig must, then, have had a minimum of forty-nine people present at his Christmas gathering. And we have been fully informed as to the precise composition of Fezziwig's guest list. You see, sir, the arrival of each and every guest has been enumerated for us by none other than your own witness, Mr. Charles Dickens:

> First came the fiddler, followed by Mrs. Fezziwig, one vast substantial smile. In came the three Miss Fezziwigs, beaming and lovable. In came the six young followers whose hearts they broke. In came all the young men and women employed in the business. In came the housemaid, with her cousin, the baker. In came the cook, with her brother's particular friend, the milkman. In came the boy from over the way, who was suspected of not having board enough from his master; trying to hide himself behind the girl from next door but one, who was proved to have had her ears pulled by her Mistress.

"Subtracting the fiddler, Mrs. Fezziwig, the three Miss Fezziwigs, their six young followers, the housemaid and her cousin, the cook, the milkman, the boy from over the way, and the girl from next door but one leaves all those employed in Fezziwig's establishment, Mr. Fezziwig included. Thus, by the power of arithmetic, my lord, we see that Mr. Fezziwig had at least forty-nine guests (and who knows if there were others not dancing the Sir Roger de Coverley) minus the seventeen singled out as not being all the young men and women employed in the business: the result, no less than thirty-two employees. So, you see, Fezziwig was a large, successful moneylender; Scrooge and Marley were too marginal to have even more than one clerk between them.

"And what sort of fellow was the clerk they had?" Tim turned toward Robert Cratchit, who sat to one side at the rear of the gallery. "Forgive me, Father, but my responsibility before this tribunal requires that I be frank." Turning back to face the judge, Tim went on, "I again recite the opinion expressed by the prosecution's star witness, Mr. Dickens, that Robert Cratchit was not a man of strong imagination."

"Perhaps," interjected Professor Blight, "your father was the best that a miser like Scrooge could or would employ, Mr. Cratchit. Perhaps he did not need a man of much imagination!"

Tim was quick to respond. "But you see, Professor, if Mr. Scrooge were a man excellent at business he surely would not have engaged and retained a clerk who lacked the imagination necessary to contribute to the assets side of Scrooge and Marley's ledger. Just as surely even a miser—nay, especially a miser—employs as many as he can to generate the profits he so hopes to hoard. Yet Ebenezer Scrooge employed only this one clerk, and he, alas, was not a very good clerk."

"How tiresome this all gets, Cratchit. Humor my good senses and tell us, if you can, how much better a clerk might Mr. Scrooge have had for the wage he paid? I daresay you will contrive to convince us that the queen's own retinue would have been a far side better off if only they'd had the opportunity to work for generous old Scrooge, ha, ha, ha!"

"I daresay I will and you'll be convinced of it too, I am quite sure. It is true enough, Professor, that we have scant ways to investigate the skills of those who might have competed for the position. But I shall endeavor to provide an earnest answer to your question, however facetious you may be in the asking. Let us but examine the wages prevailing in Mr. Scrooge's day. Was my father's salary of fifteen shillings a week the paltry income one would anticipate from a skinflint master? The answer, my lords and ladies of this court, is No! For this we have proof incontrovertible.

"I submit for the court's perusal the exhibit labeled *Wages in the United Kingdom in the Nineteenth Century*. This is the learned tome by Professor Arthur L. Bowley, published by the most esteemed and reputable Cambridge University in the earthly year 1900. His wage estimates are further supported by the distinguished researches of Dudley Baxter and Leone Levi, who arrived at entirely comparable conclusions. And what are these conclusions? Mr. Robert Cratchit, clerk to Ebenezer Scrooge, paid fifteen shillings per week, received compensation abundantly above the average. Notice, my good lord, that Mr. Bowley's estimate of average wages for highly skilled labor and manufactures, as adjusted for inflation in 1843—the year of Scrooge's ghostly visitations—was £40. For those with lesser skills the wage was £26 16s. Father earned £39 per annum, a sum comparable to that paid the highly skilled workers of his day, which—if I may so remind the court—he, being a man of little imagination, most assuredly was not. Baxter and Levi reveal that in 1843 the average weekly wage in England was betwixt eleven and twelve shillings, more than 25 percent below Mr. Robert Cratchit's salary. Thus we can conclude, my lord, that at Mr. Cratchit's wage Mr. Scrooge might have employed a well-above-average clerk. Surely we must look upon this as the record of a generous, stouthearted man." Tim, turning now to face the chief justice, continued:

"Most esteemed lord, the time has come to admit that Ebenezer Scrooge was not a miser at all. Mrs. Dilber has so testified and we have now seen that he paid my dear father, Robert Cratchit, well above the wage of a countinghouse clerk. We have seen that he did so despite the undeniable facts of his own financial circumstances. Ebenezer Scrooge was a poor, failing businessman. He lived in the decaying neighborhood of the apartment bequeathed to him by Jacob Marley. He lived on gruel even at Christmastime. His income was so meager and his business so marginal that he could not have but one employee, and an unimaginative one at that. Never can there have been a more misjudged, misrepresented, misunderstood being. At last, my lord, let us be done with this tribunal and grant him the heavenly bliss which he so well deserves."

Scrooge was very attentive throughout this speech. A raisin remained frozen between his unmoving index finger and thumb as he stared intensely from Tim to judge and back to Tim again. Perhaps the moment of his true salvation had arrived. Tim had laid a sturdy foundation for it. Scrooge, frozen in thought, betrayed a small smile.

The judge, enthralled by Tim's recitation of economic statistics, fairly beamed and glowed with delight upon hearing them. And now, obviously moved by the strength of Tim's arguments, he seemed ready to contemplate Scrooge's salvation. The gallery, though much less charmed by the dryness of inflation adjustors and per annum wages, still found much to praise in Tim Cratchit's line of reasoning. For the first time, even a majority of these spectators seemed tilted toward Scrooge's reclamation. Perhaps Ebenezer Scrooge was not a miser after all. Perhaps he had been much misjudged. He was a man with friends; a man who paid his clerk generously; a man who lived in misery and yet lived as well as he could. Oh how misjudged he seemed to have been.

Professor Blight was less impressed with Professor Bowley's learned estimation of wages in Great Britain or with Tiny Tim's peroration. Indeed, it must be said that as much as the judge glowed with enthusiasm, so much Blight glowered with antipathy.

Professor Blight interrupted before the Judge of All might speak. "Are we to conclude, Mr. Cratchit, that your poor father was a well-paid clerk and that Mr. Scrooge was a most generous employer? I say not; such a conclusion is wholly unwarranted." Blight, now looking firmly at the gallery, declared, "The honored assemblage here must not be taken in by misleading economic gobbledygook. We have only to let an economist assume a can opener, and he will claim to open all the world's mysteries before us. Nothing will be beyond his proof, whether it be that day is night or night is day. No, my friends, we must not be so easily taken in. The plain truth is that Mr. Scrooge was a mean, miserly sinner! It is but a simple matter to cast the gravest doubts on Tim Cratchit's assertions and, in doing so, to utterly destroy your momentary infatuation with Mr. Scrooge. I can myself assemble an assortment of honored and most learned professors ready to testify as to how meager a wage was fifteen shillings in London in 1843. Indeed, I have waiting in the antechamber to this very tribunal one such noted and respected authority. With the court's indulgence, allow me now to call Dr. Freddy Williams, a most honored and learned American expert, to the stand."

Dr. Williams, looking very much the twentieth-century Harvard scholar, with hat in hand and a brimming smile on his face, was

ushered into the hall by the bailiff. He carried with him volumi-
nous yellowed, cracking sheets of computerized print bearing nu-
merical information, it seemed, upon everything and anything that
might be of interest. Williams, dressed in the bell-bottomed slacks
and narrow ties of the 1970s, was wholly at odds with the mid-
nineteenth-century appearance of the court. Still, no one seemed at
all troubled by this anomaly. Blight greeted the erudite professor
most amiably. Williams's hand was grasped firmly by both hands of
Professor Blight, who proceeded to shake the unsuspecting appendage most vigorously, smiling all the while as he pumped away
at the poor witness's arm. Seeming extraordinarily jovial, Blight returned his high spirits to the subject at hand and commenced his
examination.

"Doctor, what, may I ask, is the specialty to which you have
dedicated your professional life?"

"The economic history of pay structures in Great Britain," was
the succinct response.

"And can you tell the court your view of the research by Bowley,
Baxter and Levi?"

Tim immediately objected that Blight was calling for an opinion
and conjecture. However, since Dr. Williams was a highly esteemed
authority on the subject at hand, Tim's objection was, most naturally, overturned.

"Well, I must say they were well regarded in their day, and I still
have great faith in their assessments. Their efforts were altogether
quite extraordinary."

Blight looked as down in the mouth at this news as Tim looked
pleased. But both reactions were decidedly premature, as could be
seen when Williams proceeded with his testimony. "However, the
statistics reported here from these distinguished colleagues are
quite inappropriate for the purpose to which they are being put.
These were, after all, figures for all of the United Kingdom, including the most backward and economically depressed regions, and not
just for London, where wages were, of course, much higher. Furthermore, these were general wage rates, not particularly germane
to the wage of clerks in countinghouses of the sort run by Ebenezer
Scrooge and Jacob Marley. Such data are extraordinarily difficult to

come by. Still, I have estimated wages for government clerks in Great Britain for the period under discussion. It is my considered, professional opinion that such clerks enjoyed on average an annual salary of about £235."

"Dr. Williams, are we to understand that Bowley's £40 per annum has become £235 merely by distinguishing more precisely the region and the occupation of the highly skilled laborers and manufactures?" inquired Blight with the greatest satisfaction.

"Most assuredly, Professor. You have understood me precisely. One simply cannot equate London with other places, whether it be Hull, hell, or Halifax," replied Professor Freddy Williams.

The gallery, fickle as ever, received this news with enthusiasm. Just moments before they had been all sympathy for Ebenezer Scrooge, and now in an instant they turned against him. None seemed to reflect for even a second on how easily the pendulum swung from salvation to damnation. Whether the journey back from damnation could be as easy was, of course, the issue of the moment. Surely, after the good doctor's revelations, no one would still dare to claim that Ebenezer Scrooge was a generous spirit. Apparently he truly *was* a skinflint who exploited his clerk at a most unfair wage.

Tim was devastated by Williams's testimony. Blight thanked Professor Williams, observing of the professor's testimony that "He dashes all of Tim Cratchit's claims in one stroke. Here are reported statistics not only the most dry but also the most pertinent. The good professor from America designates the salary of clerks as six times—yes, six times—greater than Bob Cratchit's pitiable income of fifteen shillings a week. So you see, Mr. Tim Cratchit, you are not alone in the study of the economics of wages. The wages quoted by my esteemed opponent are wholly inappropriate for measuring the pay of an experienced clerk such as Bob Cratchit. We have here enumerated, my lord, the correct figures. At the very cheap wage that Bob Cratchit received, it is not likely that Mr. Scrooge could have found a willing substitute. Perchance Tim's father could be replaced with an adequate clerk, but only at a much, much higher wage, making Mr. Cratchit's employment an assured bargain. Come now, ladies and gentlemen of the court, we are not such simpletons that we cannot look beyond statistical fallacies! Ebenezer Scrooge was a loathsome miser living off the fat created by the hard and ill-remunerated labor of Robert Cratchit. For this alone Ebenezer Scrooge is worthy of eternal damnation and should be so condemned this instant."

The gallery, already well persuaded of Scrooge's guilt, felt itself deeply and sympathetically impressed by Blight's call for an end to the tribunal. Blight, sensing that the moment of glory for his cause was well in hand, wheeled around to face Tiny Tim's ashen apparition. "Your witness, Mr. Cratchit."

Tim, unprepared for Professor Williams's potent testimony, appeared shattered. With one devastating number, Blight's witness had crushed the edifice of sympathy for Scrooge that Tiny Tim had slowly erected throughout the trial. He knew neither what to do nor how to go on. Having neglected to anticipate how readily his statistics could be undone, he had, with cold confidence, built toward the evidence of Bowley, Baxter and Levi with the firm conviction that they ensured Scrooge's entry into Heaven. So sure of himself had Tim Cratchit been that he had prepared no retort. Ebenezer Scrooge, with bitter, angry eyes, looked from Blight to Tim and awaited the brilliant thrust that Tim seemed suddenly so woefully incapable of providing. Tiny Tim Cratchit's plans and Ebenezer Scrooge's soul seemed to have run into a £235 stone wall.

"My God, can it be so?" babbled Tim to himself. "I cannot cross-examine, my lord. I have not been properly prepared for this witness. Time, I must have time," pleaded Tim, "time to make a reasoned response. It cannot do to examine Professor Williams just now," said Tim to the judge, and "Six times my father's wage. Good lord, six times," to himself.

Professor Blight, recognizing that Tim's march toward the reclamation of Ebenezer Scrooge had been brought to a crashing halt with one simple, devastating statistic, immediately turned toward the judge. "Most greatly esteemed Honor, is it not now clear beyond any doubt that Mr. Cratchit has utterly failed in his efforts to establish Mr. Scrooge's generosity? Can any sensible soul still doubt what we have claimed for ages past? Mr. Ebenezer Scrooge brought his miserly ways to every dealing in his life. In so doing he wreaked misery on his fellow beings, for which condemnation must now be his well-earned reward. I call upon the court to judge the facts and bring to an end these deliberations. Scrooge stands accused of being a cold, tightfisted, hard, cruel miser; this miserliness has been proved; let us have an end to it! We have tarried over this case long enough. Hellish damnation is Scrooge's rightful end!"

"Mr. Cratchit, are you prepared to cross-examine the witness, do you call a different witness, or do you make a motion to adjourn for the day?" inquired the judge most forcefully.

Tim did not respond to the judge but babbled on to himself, "Six times my father's wage, my God, six times!" Exasperated with Tim's failure to proceed and clearly moved by Williams's expert testimony, the Judge of All rose, and as it did so the court fell deathly silent. Blight's jovial smile melted away; the gallery made not a sound. The Judgment of Ebenezer Scrooge was about to be made. Scrooge, unconsciously and with great foreboding, rose to face the judge. His heavy chains rose with him, and yet not a sound did they make. Scrooge's arms enveloped the links with great care, trying to protect them from disturbing the judge. He feared the judge's silence, but not half so much as he feared the breaking of it. He wished to speak out on his own behalf; to salvage some hope for himself. But Scrooge dared not speak now! Tiny Tim, still jabbering and chattering away nonsensically to himself, began to speak to the court, uttering a half-drowned syllable as the judge's eyes imposed silence on the diminutive barrister. Both Tiny Tim's chance and the judge's patience were at an end.

The judge's arms ascended slowly, the palms embracing every corner of that great chamber, commanding the silent attention of all. The judge's lips were prepared to part when one solitary, tiny voice from a distant recess of the chamber cried out.

"No, stop, *stop!* Stop—I beg that you stop! Just give Mr. Tim until tomorrow. I know that if you will wait just one more day, we'll prove Uncle Ebenezer was not a miser. He is a kind and generous soul."

Eppie's cries stopped the court in its proverbial tracks. None had noticed the little girl's presence during the day's proceedings. She had stolen into the courtroom unseen, just as she had been

instructed. Certainly Scrooge had no awareness that she was present or that she ever attended the court or even that she knew the
way to the court. But Scrooge was sensible that there was still hope
in her loving presence, and this hope made him pull himself up
straighter and taller.

"What new testimony, little Eppie, can there be that you halt
the court now in its useful course? It seems that we have listened
attentively to all the arguments and that Tiny Tim has no more to
say. And neither, my poor dear, does your Uncle Ebenezer, or else
he would have spoken." To this Scrooge tried to interject a thought,
but—gripped by fear—he was unable to speak.

Eppie knew no such fear. "I do not know what evidence there
will be, only that Mr. Tim must remember his newspapers."

This last remark, so out of context and so out of keeping with
the solemnity of Eppie's intervention, provoked laughter in the
courtroom. Only Scrooge did not laugh.

Terrified though he was of the fate that might befall him, Scrooge
admonished the gallery for laughing at sweet little Eppie, and he
looked with such warmth and kindness on her intervention—with a
look of such love as he had not known since being separated from
his dear sister Fan—that the judge was moved by Scrooge's own display of goodness to be patient a little longer.

"This court is adjourned. We resume testimony tomorrow. At
that time a judgment will be rendered, unless there is new evidence
that warrants the trial's continuation."

Tim, Eppie, and Scrooge took their way through snow-laden streets,
down dark, still alleys, until they arrived at the gloomy abode that
might, upon the morrow, be the warmest, most comforting place
Scrooge or Eppie would ever see again.

The farther they drifted from the court, the less Tim looked to
Eppie for aid or comfort. He made every effort to dismiss her from
his discussion with Scrooge. Gently, out of respect for Scrooge's
sentiments, he suggested that Eppie eat a little dinner and go at
once to bed with her little doll.

But Scrooge demurred. "No, Tim, I think she'd better remain

with us. Was it not she, my boy, who saved the day? She has earned a place in our plans."

Tim, no longer gentle, replied, "Scrooge, what are you saying? Come to your senses now, as I have done. She must go. This girl knows nothing of our plans, of our purpose, of our objectives in Heaven. Remember who you are and what you are, Scrooge, and do as I tell you. I'll not put up with any more discussion with her. She will be our ruin!"

Scrooge, stunned by Tim's harshness, remembered once again just who he was and what he was and why Tim and Dewars and others sought his reclamation. But, Scrooge reflected, was he what and who he *had* to be? Did *he* have a choice in these plans? Was *he* compelled to serve another's purpose? Ebenezer wavered from Tim's course for a moment. Perhaps by the strength of his will he could escape the fate that lay before him. Perhaps damnation itself was preferable to the salvation *they* envisioned. Then Scrooge remembered the fearful, shrouded spirit and its outstretched finger conducting him to "salvation." "Eppie, Tiny Tim is right, my dear. You must go now and leave the planning to the grown-ups."

"Oh no, Uncle, don't listen to him. What does he care for you? What did he ever care? Listen to me, please, listen to me, Uncle Ebenezer. Repent any wrongs and God will pity you. I know that must be true even though I am only a child and not a great lawyer. Uncle, please listen to me because I love you!"

"And so do *I, Uncle* Scrooge," interjected Tiny Tim. "You have known me practically forever. Have I ever been anything but your friend and advocate? Even when I was a little child, who but I defended you when you were the Ogre of the Cratchit household? Oh Uncle, don't forget our happy past together. All I want is your salvation. And now, at last, I have the chance to do something about it, but I cannot do so when we spend our time in saccharine sentimentality for a dead little girl. Repent, indeed! There is nothing to repent. Hers is the way to false confession and damnation."

Scrooge was almost moved by Tim's appeal—almost, until he called Eppie a "dead little girl." Shaking from the cold that penetrated the cottage, Scrooge looked in anger at Tim for the first time. "What," he wondered to himself, "has happened to the sweet Tiny

Tim of Christmases long gone by? The Tim who prayed, 'God bless us, everyone.'" Still, he knew he needed the adult lawyer Tim *and* he needed Eppie, too, if he were to hold a place in Heaven. "Yes, of course, Eppie—we will both listen to you, won't we, Tim?"

Tim knew Ebenezer Scrooge well enough to recognize that the harshness with which he hoped to stun Scrooge into submission had been a poor strategy. Seeking to regain some control over the situation, Tiny Tim became as amiable as he could be. "Perhaps you are right after all, Uncle," he observed. "Perhaps the little girl could be helpful for our purpose." With that, he drew from his briefcase the newspapers that Molly had shoved into his hands.

⌧

Morning's light brought new hope to Ebenezer Scrooge. All the long night Eppie had made proposals and Tim had made proposals to achieve Ebenezer's salvation. Scrooge had hugged and kissed Eppie with each mention of how she stayed the judge's hand. All during the night's planning and deliberating his heart belonged to Eppie, his little golden idol, but his mind and soul slid steadily back under Tiny Tim's control.

Eppie, fearful of the dreaded consequences the day might bring, remained in Scrooge's poor cottage, hoping that at least she could say a final farewell to her beloved mother. No specter implored her to return to the court. She kissed her Uncle Ebenezer on the cheek, her own cheeks dampened with tears, and bade him good luck.

Scrooge and Tim, arm in arm, set off with newfound hope and optimism. Scrooge did not stop this morning, as was his wont to do, at Mr. McGreasy's shop. Tim had already been so kind as to present Scrooge with a packet of soft, chewy raisins that very morning. In short order these two gentlemen, newspapers tucked under Tiny Tim's arm, arrived at the courthouse.

The court being called to order, and the gallery eagerly expecting a judgment, the judge inquired of Tim whether he had anything new to offer that would justify postponement of the verdict. Tim, quick to his feet, indicated that he did. Restored to his confident, articulate self, Tim glowered at the gallery that had come to see Scrooge damned to hell and spoke:

"Alas for those ill-willed souls so eager to condemn Ebenezer Scrooge, the most venerable, celebrated, and revered journal, *The Times* of London, itself speaks eloquently of the bargains renounced by this gentleman in his excellent pursuit of business. It provides ample testimony of Scrooge's magnanimity and kindheartedness. It provides the foundation from which I shall proceed and from which I shall prove, at long last, Scrooge's right to eternal salvation."

"Not again, Cratchit," objected Professor Blight, this time at the edge of his seat and with his loss of patience well preserved from the previous day's session. "How much nonsense must we tolerate? What possible light might *The Times* cast upon this discussion? Certainly that worthy record made no mention of Ebenezer Scrooge, at least not in the lights of liberality and munificence. Surely by now you have understood that our beloved judge will no longer tolerate this obfuscation!"

The Judge of All interjected: "Tim Cratchit, the time of slow and deliberate development of your case is long past. Patience is at an end. If *The Times* is truly relevant, then it would be best to be out with it at once."

Tim, promising just as much haste as was consistent with his responsibilities, pressed on with cool deliberateness.

"What, surely you ask of yourselves, can *The Times* add to our discussion of wages? Within its body, little. But on its periphery, *The Times* has everything to offer. Quite literally, it offers everything. We must recall that the fashion of this great institution, in the period we discuss, was to publish advertisements of every variety within the borders of its front page. Such and such a person seeking an apartment; this or that ship sailing from Yarmouth; one or another gentleman of distinction requiring to hire a footman, a governess, a tutor, a servant, and so forth. And people of varying experience, maturity, and cultivation representing themselves before the public with regard to 'Situations Wanted.' Ah, 'Situations Wanted'! What clearer record of the availability of clerks can there be than the first page of *The Times*? Here we may examine the marketplace for clerks in all its particulars.

"A perusal of the 'Situations Wanted' during the weeks before Christmas 1843 is most revealing, my lord. Upon Christmas day we discover an experienced bookkeeper, knowledgeable in the methods of double- and single-entry bookkeeping, offering his services in exchange only for suitable board and lodging. No mention does he make of a wage."

"Stop at once, Mr. Cratchit," cried out Professor Blight. "Have you learned nothing in the day just past? You think us fools, sir. One desperate soul seeking a position means nothing, nothing at all. Come now, please Your Honor, can we not stop this man from this ridiculous course?" But before the Judge of All even looked up from its place, Tim responded directly to Blight.

"Perhaps this was the advertisement of a desperate and unusual soul. But wait, look here—in October of the same year, advertisement upon advertisement: situation wanted as a clerk in a countinghouse. Over and over again, the applicants indicate many years of experience and offer references. One gentleman 'respectably connected' reports that he 'is desirous of obtaining a situation in a countinghouse. . . . A trifling salary will be required.' Another, requesting no wage, rather reports that he can provide security up to £1,000. Yet another soul eager for employment writes, 'Wanted . . . a Situation as Clerk in a countinghouse. . . . Having been in one before, he understands bookkeeping by double entry, writes a good hand, knows town, and can have a good character. Salary only but small expected.' But none of these and the many many more can compare with the most extraordinary advertisement found in *The Times* on 4 October of the year 1843. 'Wanted . . . a Situation in a house of business. . . . The advertiser being of business habits wishes to occupy his time and would be anxious to give satisfaction. Having an income, wages would not be so much a consideration. Can give satisfactory references.'

"Remarkable, is it not, that Ebenezer Scrooge, the alleged miser, the skinflint extraordinaire, should have retained Robert Cratchit, clerk of little imagination, at fifteen shillings a week, when gentlemen of character, education, and experience were available even at no wage; *at no wage at all!*" shouted the now impassioned Tiny Tim. Regaining his normal voice, Tim smiled at the judge. "Your honored lord, there is only one reconciliation between the fact of my father's continued employment with Ebenezer Scrooge and the availability of superior substitutes at a lower wage: Mr. Ebenezer Scrooge, who is brought before us accused of miserliness, was—Professor Williams notwithstanding—a softhearted, generous, sentimental employer who would not let his employee go even when there were patently better alternatives to be had more cheaply. This was not an excellent man of business, but rather an excellent man even at the expense of his business."

Before a breath could be taken, before one syllable of suggestion could be swallowed by those gallery ears eager for an outburst from their midst, before one thought could work its way from mind to heart and back to mind again, Professor Blight jumped into the briefly silent fray. Seeing the potential of great damage done by the clever demonstration of his opponent, feeling the pendulum again swinging toward salvation, Blight sought to quickly undo Tim Cratchit's discourse.

"Mr. Bailiff, please call Mr. Robert Cratchit as my next witness."

CHAPTER SIX

BOB Cratchit entered the court. His eyes, downcast upon his entry, were never raised to meet those of any other being in the courtroom. Rather, he kept his eyes, and the head they were in, bent down as if they were in a contest with his voice to see which could be kept lower.

"Mr. Cratchit, we have heard a learned speech by your son. He has brought forward facts and figures the driest, advertisements yellowed with age and irrelevance. We know nothing whatsoever of those who offered up their services in *The Times* except that they could not find employment by more normal and sensible means. All of this is as nothing to the considerations of this court. You, sir, in your own words, must tell us of the privations you suffered at Mr. Scrooge's miserly hand," indicated Professor Blight.

Robert Cratchit, looking as if he wished he were almost anywhere else, paused in the hope of some objection to his presence or to the professor's inquiry. As none came forth, after a too-prolonged silence, he spoke. "I have had put before me a most difficult question. Mr. Scrooge, I am sure, always meant only well by me even in those early years when privation seemed to lurk in every nook and cranny of my cell. I must testify honestly that those were hard times. England was in a depression, but not half so deep as that felt by Mr. Scrooge and those in his employ. My situation was an unhappy one, providing little reward and much anguish, but Mr. Scrooge, I am sure, shared in that misery which accompanied me every day. Our offices were bare and inhospitable. So little coal was there for a fire that the meager candles illuminating our good hands were chief among the sources of heat. Mr. Scrooge's cell offered little more comfort than did mine," replied Bob.

"Aha!" interjected Professor Blight. "Mr. Scrooge's office was kept warmer than yours, then; it did offer a little more comfort—is that so, Bob?"

"Perhaps it is, counselor. To be quite truthful, yes, sir, it is so, though surely inconsequentially so. Scrooge had a very small fire, but my fire was so very much smaller that it looked, indeed, like one coal. We worked our days in perpetual cold. I am sure it was alike in other establishments—or, if not, then unavoidable in ours."

"And was your master a kind man, Mr. Cratchit?" inquired the professor. "Was he the sort who sought at every turn to lighten your burden? Or did he care so little that, as we have already heard, he coveted the coal in the box even above the retention of his loyal clerk and so forbade you to seek the warmth of an added coal on the fire?"

"It is difficult, my lord, for a man such as myself, an insignificant, humble servant in the firm of Scrooge and Marley, to judge adequately of the motives and actions of a man such as Mr. Scrooge. His business had many complications to which I was not privy, I am sure. I cannot know how to answer your question fairly without placing my own welfare in jeopardy, sir, which I am sure, sir, you would never wish me to do."

"Come now, Mr. Cratchit, you have nothing to fear from Mr. Scrooge any longer. Answer my question if you will! Did you not fear termination of your situation if you but took the coal shovel in hand?" indicated Blight.

"I should prefer not to answer, sir, thank you. I cannot answer and maintain my equanimity as the humble and loyal servant that I am and ever have been," said Bob.

"Then, if you must so equivocate, let me inquire in a different way. Was Mr. Scrooge the sort of man who would have occupied your thoughts happily upon Christmas?" asked the barrister.

"Well, Your Lordship, it was upon Christmas day that my private thoughts most frequently dwelled on Mr. Scrooge. And did I not always drink a toast in his honor on Christmas day?"

No sooner had the clerk uttered this most circumspect statement than Mrs. Cratchit, sitting in the gallery but a short distance from the reviled Mr. Scrooge, with knitting in her lap, dropped her needles and cried in exasperation, "It should be Christmas day, I am sure, on which one drinks the health of such an odious, stingy, hard, unfeeling man as Mr. Scrooge. You know he is, Robert! Nobody knows it better than you do, poor fellow!"

"My dear!" said Bob, his basset-hound eyes looking most pained by his wife's outburst. Still, Scrooge's old clerk refused to commit himself to a harsh judgment—or to any judgment at all, for that matter. Instead he temporized, indicating that his conditions of employment were hard but commenting that the job was steady and secure and that Mr. Scrooge himself labored only under slightly more improved circumstances.

Professor Blight, seeing that the witness would not declare his position but feeling well satisfied by the mood of the court, begged the clerk to step down. Tim Cratchit, not sharing in Blight's eagerness to see his father dismissed so quickly, reminded the professor that a cross-examination was still wanted. Robert Cratchit, discerning that he had not been dismissed, retook his seat and awaited any further developments.

"Father, what must follow pains me most deeply, as surely it will pain you. But justice must, for Mr. Scrooge's sake, triumph over sentimentality. Forgive me!"

"Proceed as you must, Tim," said Bob. "But know that I fear your inquiry more than anything else that has transpired in this hallowed chamber."

"For some time now we have heard testimony at cross-purposes. Scrooge was harsh; Scrooge was kind; Scrooge was cheap; Scrooge was generous. But the facts, Father—the facts will out. Christmas day 1843. Did not Mr. Scrooge *offer* you the day off with full pay?"

"Yes, my boy, he did."

"Was this the first time that he offered such a privilege to you?" asked Tim.

"Why, no. He did every year. To be sure, Mr. Scrooge was not one given to showing his kindnesses too publicly. He was quite gruff in making the offer, but I knew he meant to do well by me nevertheless."

The court found itself immediately at the establishment of Scrooge and Marley as the clock announced the close of business, Christmas Eve 1843.

> "You'll want all day to-morrow, I suppose?" said Scrooge.
>
> "If quite convenient, Sir."
>
> "It's not convenient," said Scrooge, "and it's not fair. If I was to stop half-a-crown for it, you'd think yourself ill used, I'll be bound?"
>
> The clerk smiled faintly.
>
> "And yet," said Scrooge, "you don't think me ill-used, when I pay a day's wages for no work."
>
> The clerk observed that it was only once a year.
>
> "A poor excuse for picking a man's pocket every twenty-fifth of December!" said Scrooge, buttoning his great-coat to the chin. "But I suppose you must have the whole day."

The scene returned to the courtroom, Bob Cratchit continued: "Yes, every twenty-fourth of December we had this conversation, and every twenty-fifth of December I had the day off with pay. Mr. Scrooge's lament and his crotchety manner became a joke between us. We both of us knew the final outcome of this exchange. And as certainly as the clock struck the hour, I left the office in jolly good spirits in anticipation of the wonderful celebration that would ensue at home."

"Was the day off with wages common, Father? Common, I mean, for other working people?"

"Why, no, I guess it was not, though having been so busy attending to my own affairs, I cannot really be sure," said the clerk.

"With the court's permission," continued Tiny Tim, "let us note that Mr. Robert Cratchit, clerk at Scrooge and Marley's, appears to be the only working person in all of Mr. Dickens's account of that Christmas season who was *not* working on Christmas day." With these words, the scene changed abruptly.

We but turn down the lane on which resides Scrooge and Marley, Moneylenders. The fog without makes the street no dimmer than the dimness within Scrooge's cell. There, by one faint candle's light, sits the elderly Ebenezer Scrooge upon Christmas day 1843. Alone he toils at the books of his small establishment, hunched over ledgers, fatigued from doing his day's work and that of his clerk, too. No time takes he to celebrate the occasion with a fine feast or a leisurely rest. Scrooge could no more afford to do so than he could contemplate letting his unimaginative clerk seek employment elsewhere. Scrooge's celebration is in the joy of bearing his clerk's labors. His face bears contentment as he pauses but a moment to think of how pleasant this Christmas day must be for Bob Cratchit and all the tiny Cratchits.

We depart Scrooge's establishment, where we have looked, unseen, over his toiling shoulders, and we turn onto a thriving market street. Here little children everywhere hold tight to their mothers' hands, waiting in long queues before the butcher's shop, the poulterer's, the baker's, the grocer's, and the fruiterer's. The butcher and his whole family labor long and hard to prepare all varieties of meat for their long line of customers. No time have they to catch a breath or think of their own Christmas day. Just next door the fruiterers, the grocers, and the bakers are no less engaged in pleasing the wants of their patrons, without time to tarry on the meaning of Christmas. They can no sooner close their shops in celebration of the occasion than their spirits can allow them to seek the shelter of the poor laws, in whose grasp a day's respite would plunge them. No, they—like all the working people round London—toil upon every Christmas day because they need to do so.

But a short distance away from this bustling market of fresh fruits and meats, of roasting turkeys and fine puddings, we pass by a small shop wherein seamstresses sew the clothes of fine gentlemen. There, in one dark corner, sits Martha Cratchit, Bob's eldest daughter, laboring harder than most, eager to complete her task in time to join the Cratchit household for their merry Christmas celebration. No thought has she of having all the day free from her work. No such prospect has she ever known.

Traveling yet another little distance down hills and up lanes, we pass by the lord mayor's mansion. This great man, the exemplar of London's best society, gives not a moment's thought to the labors of his fifty cooks and butlers, who work feverishly in preparing a rich feast for his guests. They have no pleasure in Christmas day, a day which is marked by longer, harder hours of sweaty labor for them than are most others. They enjoy no munificence from the lord mayor on this occasion. They receive none of the generosity so routinely consumed by Robert Cratchit this Christmas day and every other Christmas day through many long years. And so it is down every street and lane of fair London town. Everywhere are cabbies, poulterers, grocers, house servants, seamstresses, and clerks hard upon their work, Christmas day or no Christmas day. Everywhere save at Scrooge and Marley's, Moneylenders. Everywhere else!

Scrooge's old clerk continued to fix his eyes firmly on the ground, not glancing up at his diminutive son for even a minute. Tim, undaunted by his father's silence, continued. "Yes, Father, the time has come to confess Mr. Scrooge's generosity. Though he preferred to be reclusive about his giving, seeking anonymity rather than accolades, still, the time has now come to reveal his good spirit. We have just seen that you enjoyed the leisure of Christmas day without work, and now we must admit that you enjoyed additional leisure as well."

Robert Cratchit was perplexed by this latest claim. Professor Blight, seeing Tim's intention of at once discrediting his father and building the case for Ebenezer Scrooge, sat dejected, looking almost defeated.

"Father, you have reminded all present today that Great Britain was suffering a depression in the autumn of 1843. Would you say that the depression made finding work particularly difficult?" inquired Tiny Tim.

"Depressions are hard times. I cannot say how it was for others, but you yourself read advertisement after advertisement to this fine assemblage regarding poor souls in need of a situation, willing to work for practically no recompense whatsoever. That seems evidence, as you say, of the hard times."

"Ah, but Father, you did not have it so hard that you sought a new position yourself, did you? I cannot recall your seeking a situation beyond Mr. Scrooge's countinghouse. And we know you had the time to look for some new occupation."

"I beg your pardon, Mr. Cratchit," said Professor Blight, "but we know no such thing. Indeed, with Mr. Scrooge's watchful eye cast on his poor clerk, it seems most doubtful that your father could have had a moment's time for the pursuit of his own—and your—welfare."

"We do have evidence, Professor, and we do know this very thing I have said. Father, recall for the court your successful quest for a situation."

Bob Cratchit looked most perplexed indeed. Unable to fathom what Tim had in mind, he remained silent in his seat.

"Let me recall it for you and for all of us, then," said Tim. "Did not Bob Cratchit, that very Christmas on which our attention is focused, inform the entire family how he had a situation in his eye for Master Peter, my dear brother, which would bring in, if obtained, full five-and-sixpence weekly? And remember how we all laughed tremendously at the idea of Peter's being a man of business; and Peter himself looked thoughtfully at the fire from between his collars, as if he were deliberating what particular investments he should favor when he came into the receipt of that bewildering income. So, my lord, we see that Father had time enough to secure a situation for my dear brother Peter, himself but a lad with no experience whatsoever and with no references of any kind. During those hard days of depression, Robert Cratchit had time and contacts enough to find a position for Peter, and yet we are to believe that he, a man of experience, could find nothing for himself. He did not seek for himself, quite plainly, because he had a good situation that he, wisely, was loath to give up. That, Your Honor, is the reality of Robert Cratchit's employment with Ebenezer Scrooge, and high time it is, indeed, that it should be known to all."

Clearing its throat, the judge nodded affirmatively and with the faintest smile upon its face, as if to say, "Well done, Tim Cratchit."

Tim continued, "History has recorded that Mr. Scrooge was cold and hard. It has, by contrast, treated his clerk, my father, with tenderness and sympathy. Tenderness for the suffering of our family and sympathy for the difficult straits that put us in harm's way. But there are facts of my youth that are at odds with this rendition of our lives. Our Christmas feast, for instance, has been portrayed as meager and pitiful. The reality was entirely different. Our Christmas dinner was quite grand. The goose was too much to finish; every one of us had more than enough. The goose, as I recall, was magnificently accompanied by applesauce, gravy, sage, and onions and fine mashed potatoes. These fixings were followed by an inestimable pudding, the finest in all my recollection. It was a fine—and costly—meal that could not have been prepared for less than full fifteen shillings, a week's wages." As Tim spoke of the pudding, Mrs. Cratchit blushed greatly in the gallery. "But, Father," continued the son, "let us be fair and honest—the meal was but the tip of our gustatory iceberg. How well I remember, even now, that once the dinner was all done, the cloth was cleared, the hearth swept, and the fire made up. The compound in our earthen jug being tasted and considered perfect, apples and oranges were put on the table and a shovelful of chestnuts on the fire." As Tim described the meal, images of that long-past repast drifted across the consciousness of all present in the court. The scents and images, silent but profound, of the Cratchit Christmas feast hung heavily in the air.

"Come now, Father—how long can we pretend to poverty? We, a family living in our own house and with the means to serve a bowl of fresh oranges at Christmas time. Oranges, Father, in London, in 1843, in winter. Oranges, Father—oranges! The *most* expensive fruit imported into our fine city in that time, and we, a poor family? We, capable of indulging in their possession! Poor indeed! Not so poor that we could not enjoy the finest feast I can recall." These last utterances were shouted by Tiny Tim, who had, by this time, provoked himself almost beyond control.

Bob Cratchit, knowing the undeniable luxury of fresh oranges, trembled a bit in the dock. Shaken though he was, this poor soul did pull himself to his full height before speaking. "You know, you must know, that we *were* poor. How can you think otherwise? Poor we were, I daresay, yes we were—yes, poor, poor indeed!"

Tim, seemingly losing sight of his purpose in the court, proceeded to tear down his father and to establish that it was not poverty that visited want on the Cratchit household.

"I am not yet done with you, Robert Cratchit. More must be revealed if we are to comprehend fully the circumstances against which Mr. Scrooge, in his kindness, labored. That Christmas long ago, I was frail; a lame child, my withered legs encased in an iron frame. Only proper treatment, fresh air, and a meaty diet could save my life. Else, as the Ghost of Christmas Present foretold, I would die. Did my father put the money aside to insure my salvation? Did he send me to the country and fill my belly with the meat that would relieve my suffering? No! He was sorrowful, to be sure, but he was not so practical as to see a course to my deliverance. Instead, he whimpered his sympathy for my suffering, spoke boldly of my courage, and drank prodigious quantities of gin, sipping away my salvation from his mug. Even at our Christmas feast, I recall round upon round upon round of gin punch. Yes, we drank God bless us; God bless Mr. Scrooge; God bless anyone and everyone; and then drank again and again for the sake of good cheer. Spirits, oranges, and lemons endowed our Christmas repast but threatened to deprive me of the life spared only by Mr. Scrooge's generosity."

"Tim—my dear, dear Tim—how can you be so cruel and unfeeling toward your father who loved you so?" cried Bob Cratchit, sobbing into his handkerchief. "Did I not carry you high on my shoulders, letting my legs run for those little legs of yours that could not? Did anyone feel your suffering more than I, Tim? Can you be this heartless toward one who would have given everything to make you well again?" implored poor old Bob. Tim, having worked himself nearly to a frenzy, did not pause for even a breath but plunged on in his indictment of his father.

"What kind of man was this clerk, Robert Cratchit? What kind of man was the denounced Ebenezer Scrooge, the man who retained my father despite his flaws, despite his incompetence, despite his heartless cruelty? Mr. Scrooge, of course, has become known as the evil characterization of a utilitarian age. He has been wrongly accused! He was a sad and lonesome, sentimental old man, abandoned by his own father, left alone by poor, frail Fan, shunned by all but a handful of loyal friends. And who was Robert Cratchit? This man, for so long thought the victim of Scrooge's utilitarian practicality, was in fact the coldest, most self-centered, self-interested man you could ever imagine meeting. Let me take this court back to the death of Bob Cratchit's child—myself, Tiny Tim—foretold to Mr.

Scrooge by the Ghost of Christmas Present. Father had just recently returned from the cemetery where my earthly remains were consigned. Home at last from that sad setting, he reports quite tenderly the visit to that place.

"And then, all of us drawn about the fire, listening intently, Father reports the extraordinary kindness of Mr. Scrooge's nephew, whom he had scarcely seen but once, and who, meeting him in the street that day and—seeing that he looked a little . . . 'just a little down, you know,' said Bob—inquired what had happened to distress him. 'On which,' said Bob, 'for he is the pleasantest spoken gentleman you ever heard, I told him.' 'I am heartily sorry for it, Mr. Cratchit,' he said, 'and heartily sorry for your good wife. If I can be of any service to you in any way,' he said, giving me his card, 'that's where I live. Pray come to me.' 'Now it wasn't,' cried Bob, 'for the sake of anything he might be able to do for us, so much as for his kind way, that this was quite delightful. It really seemed as if he had known our Tiny Tim and felt with us. I shouldn't be at all surprised, mark what I say, if he got Peter a better situation.'

"What leapt to your mind on that cold, grey day of your life, Father? Not the great tragedy that had befallen the Cratchit household! Not the death of your own Tiny Tim! No! It was the profit that might stem from your sorrow. How your grief might be translated into more money, a few extra bob, for the family; that was what you contemplated on that bitter day! 'I shouldn't be surprised if he got Peter a better situation,' indeed! How loathsome you are. To think how you might profit from the misery that had befallen you is the contemplation of a base man."

Bob Cratchit cupped his face in his hands and sobbed. As he was led away, Scrooge reached out and pushed a very hard, dry raisin into Bob's hand. Bob smiled meekly and left the court.

CHAPTER SEVEN

WITH a resounding crash of the gavel, the judge announced the day's adjournment. No sooner had the hammer's crack finished its journey around, up, down, and through every corner of the court than the judge jumped down from the bench to join the gallery of spectators and the day's witnesses in a hot rum toddy. This surprising joviality was missed by Tiny Tim and by Scrooge, each of whom had instantly begun to leave the room on hearing the announcement of an adjournment.

Scrooge, escorted by Tiny Tim, made his way up alleys and down lanes to his tumbledown shanty. They were greeted at the door of the cottage by Eppie. She had been staring out the panes of broken window in the parlor for quite some time, awaiting Scrooge's return and news of the day's developments. Her day had been long and solitary, filled with nervous uncertainty.

No sooner had she spotted Scrooge and Tim coming down the lane than—her fear of Tim and fears for Scrooge notwithstanding—she became high-spirited and joyous. And as they drew closer, so that she could see the expressions on their faces, Eppie's feigned joy was replaced by real delight. With great pleasure, indeed, she detected that the approaching Tim and Uncle Ebenezer were themselves in high spirits. Perhaps, she thought, "Uncle Ebenezer is right to heed Tiny Tim. Maybe everything *is* going to be all right."

Not waiting for Ebenezer to say even a word to her, Eppie reached into the pocket of his greatcoat and, giggling the whole time, removed the parcel of raisins and honey that she found there while declaring that she could not possibly take hot porridge with Scrooge. Scrooge, looking down—his height and her proximity permitting him only a view of the top of her golden head—smiled warmly, albeit just a touch distantly.

Tim, no longer so worried that Scrooge would fall under Eppie's thrall, took in this scene of domestic bliss without apparent interest. His own childhood experience with cold and privation seemed not to have created any warmth within him for children similarly afflicted. But then he had not thought his childhood deprived, if we are to believe his cross-examination of Robert Cratchit. Tim neither greeted Eppie nor gave any sign of noticing her presence. However much she meant to Ebenezer, Tim cared not one whit for her. However much her salvation hung in Scrooge's balance, Tim—whose very life had once been saved by Scrooge—empathized with her not at all. For him, Eppie was an impediment to the ambition he sought to fulfill; an impediment that he feared as well as loathed. The day's successes having been many and great, Tim could feel secure in his dismissal of Eppie. He had found renewed optimism in his own abilities and lost sight of what her mention of the newspapers might suggest she knew of him and Molly.

"Uncle, tell me everything that has happened today—it seems it must be something wondrously good. Have they seen how good and kind you always were and ever after will be? Are we at last to live in Heaven forever?"

"Hush, child," replied Ebenezer. "How can I answer such a gaggle of questions when they come one after the other? Patience just a little longer, my precious. Much was good today, but no, there has been no judgment. I daresay it will come tomorrow and it will be most pleasing to us all. If nothing untoward or unexpected comes our way, tomorrow we shall all take hot porridge with raisins and honey together. Soak this parcel well, my dear, and be not stingy with the rum—let these raisins give up their shriveled form and be as plump and juicy as you are."

Eppie quite giggled and blushed at this suggestion and promised that she would do so. Her heart seemed so uplifted, so joyous, that she hopped from foot to foot as if the ground were ablaze with hot coals. Scrooge hopped about with her. All misgivings arising from the whispered fragments of conversation that had drifted through her semisleep on so many previous nights were gone like whispers in the wind. Eppie believed in Scrooge's goodness and looked forward to his freedom to be good to her, and she to him, forever more.

While Eppie and Ebenezer danced about the poor, dank parlor, Tiny Tim looked on with indifference. The private thoughts of this strange trinity—Eppie, Scrooge, and Tim—were interrupted by a knock at the door. Scrooge's high complexion faded, his smile turned toward a smirk, and he asked Eppie, still in a gentle voice, to retire to her room. "We must complete our final preparations for tomorrow, dear, and it would be best if we were left to our business uninterrupted." Eppie, disturbed by Scrooge's new manner and the smile on Tiny Tim's face, excused herself and left the parlor.

The dark shadow—the very one that had come to see Scrooge before and whose visit had been foretold by Eppie's mother—entered, it seemed, more through the door than through the doorway. It pointed Scrooge and Tim to their seats. Eppie, in her room but sensing the spirit's presence, felt warm in that cold cottage.

The specter, not knowing if Eppie was present, turned its finger toward the hearth, wherein a great fire immediately blazed. Eppie could feel the warmth radiating through her door, and in that instant she shivered with renewed fear. The atmosphere of trepidation and foreboding that had filled the house the previous two evenings engulfed her now. Had this spirit come to her the previous day for good or for ill? Inescapable terror grasped the child, clutching her toes and ragged dress, holding her by the hand and coursing through her golden hair. She feared most for the man she called Uncle. In her mind he was not associated with this dread ether upon the air but was as much a victim as was she. In the other room a heated conversation was taking place. The silent, pointing specter seemed master of the moment, although only Tiny Tim spoke. He said that tomorrow this very spirit would denounce Scrooge and in so doing would insure their plan to infiltrate Heaven, placing an unworthy soul in the midst of goodness, capturing at last that foothold from which the restoration of evil would follow. For surely the court would be moved less by the spirit's accusations than by Scrooge's repentance.

The house so filled with dread and evil that the very air was rank and putrefying. Scrooge sat at a little distance from Tim and the spirit and seemed uncertain of the terrible prospects that they contemplated. Eppie, hearing everything, clutching Molly to her bosom, feeling the blaze of the fire grow stronger, could no longer contain her fear. She cried out and in doing so washed horror and terror away. The fire in the grate died as quickly as it had begun, and the dark spirit in the other room shuddered, its commanding finger drooping before the irresistible honesty of Eppie's cry.

The shadowy spirit commanded departure from Scrooge's dwelling. Tim rose to follow but paused just long enough to counsel Scrooge to be cautious. "One more night, Ebenezer, and our work will be done. You shall find your way to Heaven, the tree of knowledge shall be picked bare, and our master shall have his own sweet reward. Just one more solitary night. Be strong, Ebenezer—be strong for one more night."

Scrooge ran to Eppie, whose tears flowed like the great rains that bore up Noah's ark. At last the flood stopped; her tears, it seemed, had drowned all evil within the lowly cottage. Ebenezer hugged the child and clung to her as if to his own salvation. How deeply he was moved by the realization that Eppie's fears were only for him—for Scrooge knew that she thought nothing at all of her own tragic fate in accompanying him wherever his soul might reside throughout all eternity. He wiped her cheek and promised her that only good could come of this evening's visit. Eppie, calmed somewhat by his assurances, inquired why there had been a fire made against all the rules. Scrooge could only answer that he did not know what power had made the fire, but it had gone out as quickly as it had risen. He suggested that this was an omen they were being watched over by a benevolent spirit that would not allow any evil to transgress against them.

More reassured than ever, Eppie told Ebenezer that she did not like Tiny Tim, that he was not so good as people thought him, that he seemed almost like an evil angel. Scrooge again reassured the child. "No, Eppie, he is very good. He is only doing his duty. A barrister must be calculating in his thoughts and behavior both inside and outside the court. Really, my dear, you must not think ill of him. He loves us both." Scrooge said this last with little conviction, but Eppie, still more assured and more calmed, gradually ceased sobbing. She picked up the book from which Scrooge had read to her on previous evenings. It fell open to a chance page, and Eppie, quite cheered now, pointed blindly at a passage and asked her Uncle Ebenezer to read from the very spot. And so he did:

> *Mephistophilis:* Why, Faustus,
> Thinkest thou Heaven is such a glorious thing?
> I tell thee, 'tis not half so fair as thou,
> Or any man that breathes on earth.
> *Faustus:* How prov'st thou that?
> *Mephistophilis:* If it were made for man, therefore is man more excellent.
> *Faustus:* If it were made for man, 'twas made for me:
> I will renounce this magic and repent.
> *Good Angel:* Faustus, repent; yet God will pity thee.
> *Evil Angel:* Thou art a spirit; God cannot pity thee.
> *Faustus:* Who buzzeth in mine ears I am a spirit?
> Be I a devil, yet God may pity me;
> Ay, God will pity me, if I repent.

They read only briefly as Eppie and Ebenezer each fell asleep, she on his lap, he with his finger still marking the spot where the good angel urged Faustus, "Repent; yet God will pity thee." Eppie's little Molly Dolly, its arms outstretched and its sock face smiling, lay just next to them, resting on the worn wool muffler Scrooge gave Eppie so long ago on Raveloe Lane.

The sun rose to a warm, harmonious day. The court filled with spectators as it had every day previous during this arduous hearing. The gallery seemed more subdued, more upstanding and decent, than on earlier occasions. This sense was shared by all present in the hallowed chamber. Its source seemed to be the young child with golden hair, sitting visible to all in her tattered dress and makeshift rag slippers, a sparkling gem among her more tawdry compatriots.

Tiny Tim, resuming where he had left off the previous day, requested that the bailiff fetch the Ghost of Christmas Present as the next witness. The ghost, who until now had sat in the gallery and not in the witness's antechamber, came forward. No time was taken in swearing this ghost to tell the truth. That he might do otherwise was inconceivable.

The spirit cut a most extraordinary figure. He was a jolly giant, glorious to see; who bore a glowing torch, in shape not unlike Plenty's horn. The enormity of his arms and their capacity to envelop all of humanity were ineffable. He was a warm and hearty fellow, and his great laugh bellowed throughout the courtroom, got caught in the rafters, bounced among them and echoed throughout the chamber, and finally came to rest in a silent heap within the ghost's beard.

Tiny Tim, appearing awed by this spirit, began his interrogation.

"Mighty spirit, I call upon you now to reveal the diabolical scheme Mr. Dickens contrived against Ebenezer Scrooge. You, above all the spirits, know this best."

"Mr. Tiny Tim Cratchit," spoke the billowy and sonorous voice of the ghost, "I believe Mr. Charles Dickens had a dark and nefarious purpose in mind when he created Ebenezer Scrooge. This author fought a mighty battle in telling the tale of Scrooge's Christmas. He struggled between fact and fiction, between truth and fabrication, between quotation and narration. The speeches of his characters portray one image of Mr. Scrooge; the personal narrative of Mr. Dickens depicts a different, less favorable portrait. Thus it was that Mr. Dickens intimated Scrooge was friendless, while you have shown him to be greatly befriended. Thus it was that Mr. Dickens implied Scrooge was a miser, while you have shown him to be a generous spirit. Thus it was that Mr. Dickens suggested Mr. Scrooge was humorless, while Mr. Scrooge joked with Marley's ghost. Did he not say, 'There's more of gravy than of grave about you'? Thus it was that Mr. Dickens altered the very record of what was said and felt by Mr. Scrooge. He suppressed fundamental evidence that showed Mr. Scrooge in a most favorable way."

"Altered the record, Spirit? Suppressed evidence?" interjected Professor Blight, by now looking quite disconsolate. "Excuse me for suggesting that as majestic a creature as yourself might have misspoken, but this is too, too horrendous a charge! Please, kindly

Spirit, enlighten us. How can Mr. Dickens—the creator of Mr. Scrooge's story—have changed the facts when he was their originator? Are there facts save those he promulgated?"

"There are facts beyond Mr. Dickens's creation, Professor. My existence and that of my brethren is not owing to Mr. Dickens; the Christmas Spirit has been known to mankind since that holy child was born in Bethlehem. I have trod upon the earth, bringing happiness where I could, suppressing misery where I could, offending no one if I could help it, for two thousand years. What did Mr. Dickens have to do with that, Professor Blight?"

"Nothing, I am quite sure," responded the professor.

The ghost continued, "I am not his creation, but the fabric of a much higher being whose purpose has ever been to help mankind. What I felt within my heart owes nothing to Mr. Dickens. Only the revelation of my utterances owes something to him. Only their revelation; not even the utterances themselves. Only their revelation and nothing more."

"Of course, holy spirit, I did not mean to suggest that *you* were Mr. Dickens's creation. But could this august author have altered your testimony regarding Ebenezer Scrooge? Indeed, was there testimony at all from you about Mr. Scrooge's character?" inquired Blight.

"With the help of my departed brother, the Ghost of Christmas Past, let this court return once again to the Christmas of 1843, to the moment in which Mr. Scrooge discovers me in the chamber next to his bedroom:

"Come in!" exclaimed the Ghost. "Come in! and know me better, man!"

Scrooge entered timidly, and hung his head before this Spirit. He was not the dogged Scrooge he had been; and though its eyes were clear and kind, he did not like to meet them.

"I am the Ghost of Christmas Present," said the Spirit. "Look upon me!" Scrooge reverently did so. It was clothed in one simple deep green robe, or mantle, bordered with white fur. This garment hung so loosely on the figure, that its capacious breast was bare, as if disdaining to be warded or concealed by any artifice. Its feet, observable beneath the ample folds of the garment, were also bare; and on its head it wore no other covering than a holly wreath set here and there with shining icicles. Its dark brown curls were long and free: free as its genial face, its sparkling eye, its open hand, its cheery voice, its unconstrained demeanor, and its joyful air. Girded round its middle was an antique scabbard, but no sword was in it, and the ancient sheath was eaten up with rust.

"You have never seen the like of me before!" exclaimed the Spirit.

"Never," Scrooge made answer to it.

The Ghost of Christmas Present rose, and as it did so Scrooge observed that at its skirts it seemed to have some object which it sought to hide. He fancied that he saw either the claw of a great bird or a foot much smaller than the Spirit's own protruding for a moment from its robes; and being curious in everything concerning these unearthly visitors, he asked the Spirit what it meant. "They are not so many as they might be," replied the Ghost, "who care to know or ask. No matter what it is, just now. Are you ready to go forth with me?"

As the last syllable faded into silence, the courtroom was restored and the ghost, lately seen in Scrooge's old chambers, was found still sitting in the witness box.

The spirit continued in his testimony: "These last few sentences you have heard for the first time, my friends. Why might that be so, if they are the true record of my meeting with Ebenezer Scrooge? Mr. Dickens deleted these words from his account of my meeting with Ebenezer Scrooge. But they were spoken by me and represented a true and higher sentiment than Mr. Dickens's deceit. I said, and I meant, that Mr. Scrooge was extraordinary in his concern for suffering. Under my robe were the children Want and Ignorance. Together, they foretold that doom which must accompany man through all his mortal days. They are the very embodiment of the travail of all humanity. They accompany me whenever I tread on the earth and mingle with the spirits of men. Your race of frail mortals strives mightily to deny the very existence of these poor children and turns a blind eye toward them. But not Mr. Scrooge. Not he! And that is why I declared then and repeat now that *they* are not so many as they might be who care to know or ask about these suffering children. Mr. Scrooge cared enough! He had barely but made my acquaintance when he noticed their presence and inquired after them. Mr. Scrooge cared enough. Mr. Dickens feared them, and he feared the caring, loving Ebenezer Scrooge. That is why he sponged these words from mankind's consciousness. He wiped them from the pages of his book. Mr. Scrooge cared enough, but Mr. Dickens strove to hide from view Mr. Scrooge's exceptional concern for his fellow beings. He altered that very record that reveals Mr. Scrooge's great goodness. You can find these words still in his original manuscript, crossed out by his own unhallowed hand before they saw the light of day."

The ghost, having completed his testimony, did not even wait for Tim or Blight to dismiss him. He soared triumphant and disappeared in a twinkling moment. With this extraordinary testimony, Scrooge's case seemed won; his salvation assured. But still Tim Cratchit was not satisfied. More evidence, stronger evidence, must see the light of day before he would relent and permit the court to conclude its deliberations. Professor Blight sat silently at his great desk, his depression and dejection seeming insurmountable yet mingled with admiration for Tiny Tim's supreme accomplishment. Scrooge's enemies were already departing from the gallery, unable to bear any longer the litany of evidence that was crushing their hopes of his condemnation. They hated him still. Even now they suspected some evil intention behind the image of Scrooge portrayed to the court.

Tiny Tim requested that Mr. Jacob Marley be called to address the tribunal. Bailiff Dickerson complied immediately.

Marley's ghost, ashen in color and sullen in appearance, approached the dock. The specter wore spectacles on its forehead as if to contain its hair, which was ever in motion. The translucence of his form was, even in this gathering, a frightful sight. So woeful a creature as Marley's ghost was a painful vision to behold. Those remaining in the gallery turned away in horror, unwilling to cast their eyes upon this lost soul, returned from hell to testify before the awesome court.

Marley took his seat slowly, having first to arrange the ponderous chain he was compelled to bear. Scrooge, who bore an equally ponderous chain, gasped at the sight of his dear friend. They had not been permitted to meet one another these more than six score years since Scrooge had departed his earthly realm. He, alone among all those observing the deliberations, reached out to grasp Jacob's hand, but he was prohibited by the bailiff from succeeding in this endeavor.

"Jacob Marley, we have heard testimony that you and the accused, Ebenezer Scrooge, were kindred spirits in life. Is this so?" inquired Tim.

"Yes, it is," the ghost replied in a droning voice.

"And Jacob, can we infer, then, that whatever may be said of you may be said of Scrooge as well?"

"Yes" droned the ghost, "and what may be said of Ebenezer, poor soul, may also be said of me!"

"Jacob, your testimony, above all, is most crucial. You alone can establish my original claim that Ebenezer Scrooge was more than merely good, kind, and generous; you can prove that he, like you, was saintly—truly saintly."

This contention caused an outcry in the gallery. Marley's ghost, unlike Scrooge's, had already been condemned to eternal wandering, eternal torment, the eternal torture of remorse. The chains that fettered him could not easily be undone. There was scant hope of salvation left for him. How, then, could Tiny Tim Cratchit claim saintliness for this specter? It was a blasphemous outrage that the gallery refused to tolerate. A violent, chaotic uproar arose, with hoots and cries of "No! No! No!" The Judge of All, stirring in its seat atop the high podium, raised an outraged finger at the gallery. Instantly, the revilers of Marley and Scrooge fell silent. The judge reminded all present that Tim could make any claim without fear.

"Thank you, my lord." Tim said haughtily. "Here, above all places, no being must dread speaking the truth. We should not rashly hold an opinion in so weighty a matter, so that we may not come later to hate whatever truth may reveal to us, out of love for our own error."

"Jacob, what circumstance brought your spirit to visit Ebenezer in his mortal form that Christmas long ago?" inquired Tim.

"I was not permitted then to tell Ebenezer, but here I may say that an angel sent me to him."

"An angel, Jacob? For what purpose?" asked Tim.

As Marley's ghost prepared to answer, the courtroom was again conveyed, though only for a moment, to Scrooge's chambers, where, trembling in a hard, uncomfortable chair, wrapped in a threadbare blanket, Ebenezer Scrooge's long-past self sat listening to the spirit of Jacob Marley.

> "I am here to-night to warn you, that you have yet a chance and hope of escaping my fate. A chance and hope of my procuring, Ebenezer."

Tim inquired how easily mortals lost the opportunity of such salvation as Jacob had offered Scrooge. After all, noted Tim, Scrooge seemed unique in being given this chance through angelic intervention.

Jacob replied that Scrooge's circumstances were most wondrous; that mortals normally lost the opportunity of redemption most easily. "Indeed," he said, "the grapes of wrath hang heavy on heaven's vine; the fruit of forgiveness is rarer still than the sweet nectar of the gods." Being pressed to clarify his meaning, Jacob said that He who had sent him in the spirit of Christmas had instructed him to inform Scrooge that "no space of regret can make amends for one life's opportunity misused," and, Jacob went on to observe, he had prayed often that Scrooge would heed his warning and so be saved.

"No space of regret, Jacob? Are we to understand you told Ebenezer that to have misused a chance to do good even once was sufficient to be damned forever? That *no space of regret* could make amends for *one* life's opportunity misused?"

"Yes, it is so," murmured Marley's ghost. "Oh woe to those who squander their chance. Woeful, endless damnation for those who fail to heed any little opportunity to help their fellow beings. Torment, torment, tor–ment is their everlasting, incessant companion." As Jacob uttered these sentiments, he rattled his chains in a wild, contorted ecstasy of suffering.

"Oh Jacob—calm yourself, Jacob—you were always a good man," interjected Scrooge. Tim, with a finger to his lips, silenced Ebenezer and then proceeded in his questioning of Jacob Marley.

"Then, Jacob, if there was yet a chance and hope for Ebenezer Scrooge, he must not yet have misused even one life's opportunity! That old man—for he surely was old when you last visited him—had lived so pure—nay, let me say, *saintly*—a life that he had not yet failed to seize life's opportunities to do good even once. Is that not so?"

"It must be so if I could do him any good," answered Marley's ghost.

"And you, Jacob—what manner of man must you have been?"

"I tried to be good, sir," answered Marley meekly.

"More than good, Jacob. You, too, must—like your good friend Ebenezer—have been saintly." The apparition seemed perplexed by this characterization, so Tim continued, "Yes, Jacob, you—saintly! Did you not intervene for the good of Ebenezer Scrooge, though your spirit could derive no benefit from the intercession? You, who are condemned forever, acted out of the highest altruistic motive to save your dear friend from your wretched fate. And have you not asked yourself, Jacob, how it was that *you* had this power to intervene for good? Do you recall what you told Scrooge those many years ago about the phantoms that you revealed to him—those specters seen suffering just outside the window of his bedchamber at the moment of your departure?"

"Yes," said Jacob quizzically, "I do remember. I said, 'The misery with them all was, clearly, that they sought to interfere, for good, in human matters, and had lost the power forever.'"

"Yes, Jacob, that's it! They had lost the power forever, but you had not. You had *not* lost the power. You, blessed Jacob—like Ebenezer Scrooge, your kindred spirit—you, too, had not misused even one life's opportunity; you, too, sought only to be beneficial to your fellow human beings," proclaimed Tiny Tim. The Judge of All smiled compassionately at the long-condemned remains of Jacob Marley.

Marley then inquired sadly, "If what you say is so, how is it that Ebenezer and I are both fettered in chains?"

Tim replied, "Poor Jacob, when your soul was placed on trial, you had inadequate council. You and Ebenezer, kindred spirits that you were, were persecuted with chains because of misguided prejudice against your religious convictions. Neither of you, we must recall, observed Christmas. You cannot have been Christians, then; yet you both were faithfully devoted to God. Is it not true that Ebenezer but once referred to God in *A Christmas Carol* and that once was in defense of his beloved sister Fan? Surely he did not then take the name of God in vain and, just as surely, neither did you. No, Jacob, you and Ebenezer were fettered by unjust prejudice, and you were condemned because your barrister was too ignorant to have noticed it. But this court can undo the injustice done you. This court and this judge know no religious prejudice but love only a life well lived."

The revelations brought forward by Tim's interrogation of Marley's ghost were most amazing. The evidence had been there all along. Within the confines of Dickens's own account, the truth lay lurking. Surely there was yet a chance and a hope for Ebenezer Scrooge, and perhaps even for the wrongly condemned Jacob Marley. The truth will out!

Marley's testimony had greatly moved the court. How much sympathy there was now for Ebenezer Scrooge cannot be said. That it was inestimably large there can be no doubt—no doubt whatsoever. Now that all seemed ready to forgive Scrooge and even to sanctify his holiness, Mr. Charles Dickens entered the chamber and begged sufferance to speak one last time.

The Judge of All acquiesced. The author, garbed in a flaming red suit, his appearance most bizarre and even frightening, his hair greatly agitated, spoke in tones that roared throughout the hall, crashing on the oak pillars and setting them into vibration. He veritably cried out that "Ebenezer Scrooge must be condemned for his sins!"

This prompted immediate hissing from the gallery, which the judge silenced instantly. Dickens continued, "Ebenezer Scrooge must be condemned for all eternity. He has sold his soul; he has made a pact with the very devil; he has extracted his reward, and he must not escape his punishment. Most awesome Judge, hear my testimony and heed my plea. This sinner must be condemned."

Professor Blight was paralyzed into silence by the ghastly likeness of Charles Dickens that was before the court. All eyes were on this apparition, else they might have noticed the surprisingly placid look on Tiny Tim's face. At last Blight recovered and rose to parry Dickens's thrust.

"Sir," he shouted, "what is this nonsense you bring before the court? How dare you waste our time with the rambling idiocy of a discredited madman! We all see now the evil you have done; we all see now the contemptible plot you set for us and for Scrooge; we all see now what the truth is and what must be done."

"No," retorted Dickens's ghastly ghost, "You see nothing; it is you who are mad, you who are blind. I admit that Mr. Scrooge was saintly *before* his visitations. That others have not previously seen this I cannot help. He was made saintly for the very purpose of his condemnation. That saintliness is what made him so wonderful an object for the devil. To destroy an old soul that had not transgressed even once was a marvelous challenge. Yes, I admit as much. Scrooge had led an exemplary life. True, his publicly declared sentiments were often crass and cruel in sound. Did he not say of Christmas that 'If I could work my will every idiot who goes about with "Merry Christmas," on his lips, should be boiled with his own pudding, and buried with a stake of holly through his heart. He should!' But actions, my lords, must speak louder than words; Scrooge's actions were generous and kind, if sometimes very private and invisible to those who would not look closely to see. He had not been the sort who gave generously in order to imbibe the gratitude of the needy. He gave because it was good to give, especially good when it was done without the beneficiary's knowledge and even without his knowing who the recipient was." In this he observed faithfully the Talmudic teaching of what constitutes the highest, holiest form of charity: to give with no prospect of reward.

"Then," interrupted Professor Blight, most curious about Dickens's intercession, "why are you here pursuing Scrooge's damnation? How can you accuse this man of being a sinner? You contradict yourself, sir! Was he a saint or was he a sinner?"

"Blind fools! Don't you see?" continued Dickens's ghost. "He revealed his frailty and his sinfulness that Christmas Eve of which I wrote. That was the very message of my little book. Let the Ghost of Christmas Yet to Come, the angel Mephistopheles, testify, my lord, and all will be clear."

The Judge of All nodded his assent, although the prospect of *this ghost's* presence in these sacred halls made all others tremble with fear. The phantom slowly, gravely, silently approached, the very air through which it moved scattering gloom and mystery. It was shrouded in a deep black garment that concealed its head, its face, its form, and left nothing of itself visible save one outstretched hand. But for this it would have been difficult to detach its figure from the night, to separate it from the darkness by which it was surrounded. The specter entered the box but did not sit. The court shuddered, all except for Tiny Tim, whose lips curled upward ever so slightly at the sight of the fearsome specter.

"Grave spirit, glorious Angel of Darkness," spoke the apparition of Charles Dickens, his voice now falling to a barely audible hush, "did you not reach an accord with Ebenezer Scrooge—a compact for his soul?"

"That was my purpose in dealing with the man you call Scrooge. Ebenezer Scrooge has promised his soul to my master, who has fulfilled his promise to Scrooge. The soul must be ours."

"What was that promise?"

"Ebenezer Scrooge loved himself in life. Confronted with his mortality, his only thought was to prolong his corporeal, mortal form. To this end Scrooge struck a bargain—a bargain that would grant him an increased reign in the mortal realm; an extension to give him life a little longer. For the prize of life he promised to change in outward appearance. He abandoned his repugnant motives of munificence, altruism, charity, generosity, and liberality, which marked his days before our meeting. He promised from that time forward to do good not out of a righteous desire for the welfare of others but out of selfish motives. He would replace generosity to others with greed for his own well-being. He would do this for the devil; he would grant his soul everlasting to my master, and Scrooge would be granted a longer life in his mortal existence. Remember the words he spoke to me when long ago I escorted him to the site of his own gravestone, when he at last was confronted with his mortality: 'Assure me that I yet may change these shadows you have shown me, by an altered life! I will honor Christmas in my heart, and try to keep it all the year. I will live in the Past, the Present, and the Future. The Spirits of all Three shall strive within me. I will not shut out the lessons that they teach.'" The spirit's voice rose, and the index finger of its left hand—its one exposed appendage—rose with it: "'*Oh, tell me I may sponge away the writing on this stone!*' He was so assured. The words would be sponged away from the stone; life would be prolonged, but a price must be exacted and he accepted that price. His soul is ours, and we have come to claim it. I remind this court now that no space of mortal regret can make amends for one life's opportunity misused. No space! This man Scrooge devoted his eternity to the service of my master. We have stricken from him all generosity of spirit. Tempted by the tree of life, he has succumbed. Scrooge has forsaken his eternity. We have given him his reward, he has abandoned his astonishing goodness for our sake and his, and we now claim our rightful property in his damnation."

Scrooge, now more fearful of the pendulum's swing than ever before, jumped to his feet, his eyes pinched almost shut, his whole body and soul trembling, his chain clattering and clanking horrendously. "I did not know what I was doing. I had been truly good. I fulfilled the expectations of the Ghosts of Christmas Past, Present, and Future. Was there only to be betrayal now? Am I not to receive the reward foretold by these specters? Had they not come for my welfare, and have I not earned that welfare by my righteousness? Can the words truly have been sponged away if I am denied salvation now?"

The Judge of All frowned at Scrooge's self-pitying pleas and shook its great head harshly.

"Ebenezer Scrooge, you will be told for the last time, the last time *forever*, that you must not speak out in this court whenever the time suits you. Be silent!"

And then Tiny Tim spoke out most astonishingly: "Oh Ebenezer, what have you done? How can you be saved when such a lowly, evil bargain has been struck? I pity you, yes, but I cannot—nay, I will not—save you now!"

Scrooge, hearing Tim, seemed seized with calm where trembling terror had reigned only a moment before. Seeing all hope vanish with the testimony of the darkest specter, Scrooge was undaunted even by the judge's threats. With anger and contempt in his eyes, he continued in his own defense. The judge leaned forward to silence Scrooge and then, thinking better of it, decided to hear what Scrooge had to say.

"Too long have I been compelled to sit in idle silence, listening to jibes and jeers and taunts and taints of my spirit. Too long have I had no consolation but to listen to venomous lies from all who would be filled with glee at my damnation. Too long, but not any longer! This court has learned full well of that charity which I chose to hide in life. This court has learned full well of that sentimentality for Bob Cratchit and all the little Cratchits that lay sheltered in my heart all my life. This court has learned full well the man I was and wished to be!

"Only once in the great span of my mortal existence did I falter. Only once! And even then, my sinning lay in the good deeds that I did. Yes, to do good deeds—that was the sin for which I now face damnation. Merely for doing good deeds in such a way that I might benefit from them, too! What was my choice, I ask you now, even as I know that you are not capable of feeling any pity for me."

The judge winced at this suggestion but spoke not at all, allowing Scrooge to continue in his own defense or to seal his own fate. Scrooge did so, with contempt rising in his voice and all awareness of what he might be doing to Eppie vanished from his consciousness.

"The quiet humility that accompanied my lifetime has brought me only contempt and ostracism from the paths of my fellow beings. What use had I for that humility which brought me only misery and forged for me only this chain that I bear proudly now? What use has any human being to bear the hateful wrath of others in innocent silence? What use? What use?

"An old and lonesome man was I when the Christmas ghosts scorned me and startled me into a changed life. How often I said after their time had passed, 'I'm not the man I was,' I cannot tell. But truly, I was not the man I had been. I was changed—not for the better and, I pray, not forever. But however I was changed, whatever outward alteration there had been that masked the humbler doings of my earlier time on earth, whatever these changes were and whatever they have meant to this court, they were the reactions of an old and lonely man terrified by the presence of the spirit world. My heart did not melt before the Ghost of Christmas Yet to Come; how could any heart melt before such a cold, dispassionate specter? But fear that specter I did and do even now, even as many in this court have shuddered at its presence. How can any just God condemn a man for fearing a spirit whose essence scares the very souls of those already in Heaven? What kind of God would ignore a lifetime of care and concern because a forlorn, forsaken, unloved old man sought some small solace, some small hope of time to become unfettered for his eternity? If this be the God of Heaven, I care not for it. If this be the God of Heaven, I cannot repent to it! Send me to hell, where I may know rest and justice at last!" Scrooge sat down.

Little Eppie surged forward. The dark specter, seeing her goodness, cringed, its sinister finger rolling back into the protective shield of its shroud. She ran to the defendant's box and clutched Uncle Ebenezer around his legs where her little arms could reach. He bent down to her, his heart softening and his eyes filled with tears—tears not for himself but for the sadness in her eyes and for the realization that she, too, because of the promise made him long ago, was damned. He reached out and took this good little angel in his arms, lifting her to his bosom and hugging her tightly, stopping her tears as his were given the freedom to flow unencumbered. Little Eppie kissed Ebenezer on his cheek. He, trembling again, now fearing his imminent condemnation and once again valuing the Heaven whose entry he had just decried, grasped her closer to him. Eppie looked up into his eyes and whispered, "Uncle Ebenezer, repent; yet God will pity thee."

Scrooge, still holding Eppie, clutching her as if for all eternity, took in every face and frown in the courtroom. He was perplexed, that was clear enough. He looked briefly at his creator, marveling at the horrendous taste that could have produced Charles Dickens's now comical look in his fiery red suit. What thoughts flew through Scrooge's mind as he witnessed Dickens's hissing, twisting, hateful looks we shall never know. His eyes fell upon Tiny Tim, once the sainted child who had prayed that God might bless everyone. The innocence of youth that still accompanied Tiny Tim at the trial's beginning had long departed. Scrooge saw in him now only a hardened, grasping, covetous advocate. Tim had become a man who knew no bounds, no sentiment of human decency in his dealings with his fellow beings. He had sought Scrooge's salvation not out of love for Ebenezer or for any worthy cause but only for his own nefarious aims, with no regard for righteousness and justice. Laura Dilber, sweet Mrs. Dilber, smiled at Scrooge even as she made ringlets of hair round her busy, worried fingers. Professor Blight, half standing and half seated, received a little smile from Scrooge but seemed uncertain whether his station and the circumstances called for him to return the favor or look darkly at Scrooge. Ebenezer's eyes came to rest at last, and frighteningly, on the shrouded figure of the Ghost of Christmas Yet to Come. The dark specter leaned forward, its long finger unfurled and seeming again strong and confident, beckoning Scrooge. The specter's shroud melted into the form of Molly—uncovering its true self—as it repeated Eppie's words: "Repent; yet God will pity thee." Stunned and uplifted by this metamorphosis, Scrooge turned so that his eyes fell on the Judge of All. The judge, now dressed in rags and assuming the very image of the ancient biddy who sat with her mangy dog in front of St. Paul's lo those many years ago, waited for Scrooge to speak. Ebenezer, struggling to gain sufficient composure to be comprehended and fallen upon his knees, little Eppie and Molly, revealed as the good angel she always was, now at his side, addressed the Judge of All: "Be I a devil, yet God may pity me; ay, God will pity me, if I repent. I *do* Repent! God forgive me, I repent!"

Tiny Tim, against his own best judgment, revealing the evil within him for all to see and hear, shouted out, "God cannot pity thee!"

The judge looked upon Ebenezer Scrooge. The courtroom fell silent. Tim, Scrooge, Blight, and all the rest waited motionless, breathless, as the Judge of All, looking into Scrooge's heart for one last time, commanded:

"I will pity thee. I do pity thee. Get thee to Heaven!"

Gently, Scrooge set Eppie down, took a plump raisin from his pocket, and ate it. As he did so he smiled. The gallery, with much

hoopla and clanking of tankards, slowly drained from the courtroom. Scrooge now cast his eyes beyond the gallery, beyond Molly,
beyond Tiny Tim, beyond Charles Dickens, beyond the court, beyond the memory of his beloved sister Fan, beyond Eppie, beyond
the Judge of All, and looked into the shadow of eternity. He turned,
and hand in hand with Eppie and with Tiny Tim, with wandering
steps and slow, through Heaven took his solitary way forever.

The End

Epilogue

THE TRIAL OF EBENEZER SCROOGE certainly depicts the main character of *A Christmas Carol* in an unaccustomed light. I have portrayed Scrooge as arguably a generous, thoughtful man, befriended by many and deeply concerned about the welfare of others. Yet his representation is wholly consistent with much of the direct evidence presented in Charles Dickens's fine book. Virtually all of the testimony I present here is either drawn from Dickens's account or is an accurate reflection of the times. Indeed, one may well wonder whether Dickens was conscious of the duality between his own narrative and the quoted statements of his characters regarding Ebenezer Scrooge. Perhaps we have misread his story for more than a century and a half.

The life of Ebenezer Scrooge bears much resemblance to the tale of Faust. In fact, the book Scrooge reads to Eppie is Christopher Marlowe's *Dr. Faustus*. Throughout Dickens's great work, Scrooge resists the message of his ghostly visitors, objecting that he is too old—that they should seek a worthier subject. Only when he contemplates his own mortality does Scrooge firmly commit himself to a changed life in return for a postponed death. Confronting the Ghost of Christmas Yet to Come, Scrooge pleads, "'Oh, tell me I may sponge away the writing on this stone!' In his agony, he caught the spectral hand. It sought to free itself, but he was strong in his entreaty, and detained it." Before this encounter, however much Dickens strove to cast Scrooge in a bad light, it must be admitted that significant evidence exists to prove that Scrooge was meritorious. Recall that Scrooge still had a chance at salvation even though his late partner, Jacob Marley, tells Scrooge that "no space of regret can make amends for one life's opportunity misused."

The recitation of data on wages in England in 1843 is an accurate accounting. Only Professor Williams is a fictionalized character. His testimony that the wage for clerks was about £235 per annum is based on recent research on wages, though that research has been criticized for its small sample. It is likely that Bob Cratchit's wage, as suggested by Bowley's data, was about average. Furthermore, the advertisements quoted from *The Times* of London are all authentic, suggesting that Scrooge could have secured the services of a well-qualified clerk for little or no wage. In this regard it should also be noted that oranges were the most expensive fruit available in the London market at the time and that the Cratchit feast was judged lavish even by contemporary readers of Dickens's tale.

Most of the characters in my story are drawn directly from *A Christmas Carol*. Mr. Fezziwig, Dick Wilkins, and Ali Baba are all depicted in fairly faithful accordance with the evidence drawn from Mr. Dickens's book. The faithfulness of testimony applies quite generally to the text, including the claim by the Ghost of Christmas Present that Scrooge was particularly observant of the children Want and Ignorance. Indeed, the passage quoted in my text is drawn directly from a facsimile of the original manuscript that Dickens edited just prior to publication.

Eppie is the only significant character wholly fabricated here. She is, of course, an amalgam of the Eppie of *Silas Marner* and of Tiny Tim as he appears in *A Christmas Carol*. Even Professor Blight and Hiram Dewars, though not given names in *A Christmas Carol*, are drawn directly from characters in that book. They are, as noted in the court testimony, the two friends of Scrooge who are seen discussing the disposition of Scrooge's wealth in Stave IV of Dickens's novel. Tiny Tim, of course, is the most transformed character. As Eppie can substitute for the sweet Tim of *A Christmas Carol*, so Tim can substitute here for the seemingly unfeeling, uncaring Scrooge of that same book.

We now know that Tiny Tim suffered from a form of renal acidosis, a disease that lacked a name in Tim's time but whose symptoms and treatment were well known. Sunshine, fresh country air, and a high-protein diet were known to eliminate the progression of the disease and spare the life of its victim. This simple treatment makes the Cratchit household's penchant for drink and lavish meals all the more troubling. It is unlikely that fifteen shillings per week was sufficient both for such a Christmas feast as they had and for a high-protein diet for Tiny Tim. Evidently, the family chose the former over the latter.

I have taken great care not to create important evidence on Scrooge's behalf out of whole cloth. Indeed, much additional evidence in support of Ebenezer Scrooge could be presented, including evidence that his persecution represents the anti-Semitism prevalent in England in the 1840s. In this regard the interested reader might contemplate the meaning of the term *Walker*, which is used by the young boy whom Scrooge pays to fetch the prize turkey from the butcher down the street in the original story. This term, accompanied by the thumb's touching the nose and the other fingers' wiggling animatedly, was an anti-Semitic slur of the 1840s. Dickens used this very gesture whenever he came to that passage of his book in his public readings. Its meaning, lost to the modern reader, would surely have been clear to Dickens's contemporaries.

My purpose has been to raise just a little our sympathy for Ebenezer Scrooge, a man who passed a lonely childhood and who may have been much kinder and more generous than we have previously thought. But then, we should not forget Milton's final line in *Paradise Lost* as we remember that in the end Scrooge, hand in hand with Eppie *and with Tiny Tim*, with wandering steps and slow, through Heaven took his solitary way forever.